I0769502

Editor: Krysta Winsheimer of Muse Retrospect

Book Design: Run Amok Books

Cover Photograph: Vern Smith

Cover Design: Matt Phillips

ISBN: 979-8-9904851-4-3
Run Amok Crime, 2025
First Edition

Run Amok

Printed in the USA

»»»»»»

SECOND LIES
the SON

»»»»»»

Matt Phillips

I'm about as nothing as you can get. What's that mean? Well, I'm halfway dead already, standing right where I am—you ever hear a dead man's story? Hell, it's a first for me. And you know what they say about the first: It shall be last. Oh, yes it shall. I'm out here in the sun, and I keep hearing FNG's shovel hit the dirt.*

It's like a rotten tooth piercing apple skin.

Plunge. Toss.

Plunge. Toss.

FNG over there is digging himself a foxhole. Behind the wire, too. Talk about paranoid. You want to know what that stands for, right? FNG? Fucking new guy. Another clever-ass acronym from your favorite small-town Marine, thank you very much. Where was I?

I was telling you how I don't exist.

I was saying—in so many words—that I'm dead.

Toss. Plunge.

Oh, this skinny FNG.

I was saying that I'm nothing. That I never was. Maybe I'm being dramatic, crying about a whole bunch of bullshit that doesn't deserve one bucket of salty tears. Fine, call me on it. But don't you say my story isn't worth a damn. I went through the thing. And I deserve a word or two. Like my old man used to say, when it comes to stories, they got all kinds.

In this story, you might hear a gunshot or two.

See some blood spilled.

And, look, I want to tell you to ignore all that, to see all these people as good, fine characters. That's what they want to be—it's what we all want to be. But the truth is more complicated than that, more complex. And where those smooth places ripple up like landscape is where this story lives. It's told from the bumps and gullies—it's told from the dirt. You can smell it. You can feel it on your face. When you finish this one, you might need a deep scrubbing.

And yeah, fine, it's an American story.

You think there's something wrong with that?

I sure as hell don't. I think that's the whole point.

Look, I'll tell you how it is:

Out here, nobody gives two shits for ideals. Nobody plays politician. All that stuff disappears when you get a lightning show of tracer fire every night of the week. We're not professors or pundits. We're men—a bunch of guys who want clean fucking underwear. And a hot shower. And more ammo. Can't ever have too many bullets—that's the first thing I learned.

You can never have too much ammunition.

Plunge. Toss.

Plunge. Toss.

FNG keeps digging. Thinks he's going to make it through this war. What he doesn't know is this: None of us are going to make it. We're all goners—this thing is going to change us. You start one way, and you end up another. That's the deal. It's the interest you owe.

Toss. Plunge.

Ain't no winners in foxholes. None that I ever met.

I walk over and FNG is sweating to the gills.

I tell him the hole won't save him. Matter of fact, FNG is digging himself a grave. He's pretty pissed. Gives me a killer's look. That's alright. I've seen the look before. You know the one: shiny, unblinking eyes, crow's-feet clinching down along his cheeks, a fault line running from nose to brow. "Look at this FNG," I say, "doing us all a favor and digging his own grave." I tell him he's sweet, that I appreciate his can-do attitude. Semper Fi, motherfuckers.

FNG might make a good Marine after all—he might just make one hell of a Marine.

Toss.

Plunge.

"Don't let me slow you down," I say. *"I'm already dead."*

Toss.

"Hell, FNG, I can walk through walls. Can you walk through walls?"

Plunge.

"That's what I thought. See me, FNG? I don't exist."

I'm nothing.

Toss. Plunge.

"And so are you, FNG. So are you."

PART I
Troublemakers

1

Too few dreams, and a man thinks himself lost. Have the same dream too many times, and a man knows he's lost.

The dream Sam had—again and again and again—was about his father.

At least, he thought it was about his father. But when the dream kept coming, when it resurfaced in his mind night after night, Sam began to think the dream was about something else. What that something else was, he didn't know.

The dream started like the truth:

The last time Sam saw his father was on an August Sunday, a week before starting the sixth grade. They were outside the trailer, beside his father's green pickup truck. His father was sunburned on the back of his neck and elbows, his thin shoulder blades blush red in the afternoon sun.

"Like this," he said to Sam, "a fraction at a time." He lifted a silver wrench with grease-stained fingers and ducked his head beneath the pickup truck's hood. His elbow levered up and down as he wrenched on some vague engine part. He grimaced. Sweat ran down his forehead, gathered in beads along his collarbone.

Beside the man, barefoot in the dirt, Sam Carl held a hammer. It was heavy in his hand, and it was heavy tapping against his thigh. It was his hammer, the one his father gave him four years prior for his seventh birthday.

"Like that?" Sam asked. He hefted the hammer, rested it on his shoulder.

"That's right," his father said. "Little by little, Sam—that's how a man gets things done in this life. You grind it out, and it squeaks out clean in the end." He grunted at the resistant part beneath the hood. "Come on, you son of a gun. Get out of there." He tugged harder on the wrench. Bore down on it like a man carved from granite—the engine part gave way, and the wrench slammed against metal with a loud clang. "There it is," he said. He handed Sam the wrench and dipped both hands into the engine, came out with a metal piece shaped—from what Sam could tell—like a heart. It was black and covered with grease, but with tubes and wires running off it like torn tendons. "Finally came out, didn't it?"

To Sam, the part looked foreign and mysterious, like a weird body part from one of the horror films he sometimes watched without his mom's permission. "What in the hell is it?"

"Another damn broken part—that's what the hell it is."

"Why'd it break?" Sam stood on his tiptoes, let the weights of the wrench and hammer dangle from each hand. He swung the tools back and forth above his knees. The shifting weight made him feel locked in place, as if his feet were stuck to the dirt beneath them.

"Got run down to nothing, probably. All busted up. Hell, everything breaks. Everything you see has an end out there somewhere." He turned the part in his hands, squinted at the small dark places where the wires ran into it. "You can't know when it is, but the end is always on its way."

"The end is always on its way?" Sam said this as a question, but it wasn't a question for his father to answer. It was a question to say he understood, that Sam—at eleven years old—understood endings even as he was beginning his adult life. This Sunday afternoon in late August might have been the first true ending in Sam's life, the day he understood everything was impermanent—the whole world was always hurtling toward an end. Distant, maybe. But an end however you looked at it.

"You going to fix the truck, Dad?" Sam watched his father's face for a reaction.

"I think this whole truck is dead," Sam's father said. "It's empty, like a bone you find in the desert. Nothing else inside it."

Sam turned to the truck. He lifted the hammer and swung it as hard as he could at the brittle yellow plastic covering the headlight—the hammer slammed through the hard plastic and shattered pieces onto the dirt.

"The hell you doing, boy?" A hand slapped the back of Sam's head, and he felt the familiar tingle of pain run down his neck and into his shoulders.

"You said it's dead," he said without looking at his father.

"Damn you, Sam. Always breaking things, like it's a brittle fucking world."

Sam stared at the plastic pieces shattered around his feet. He thought, *Brittle means it's easy to break.* When he turned to look at his father, the man's reddened back was turned—he was walking toward a low-hanging sun, the black heart from inside the pickup dangling from one hand.

"Dead," Sam said to himself, "means it's never coming back."

And if the dream ended there, it would have been the truth.

It would have been fact, pure and certain fact.

But his dreams, Sam discovered, never ended—not once— with the truth.

»»»»»

If you knew the light well enough—those shades of night slipping into dawn—you could tell the time without a clock. By the way the morning light came in through the window, how it danced off the picture frames on the far wall and seeped into the worn carpet. And you'd know whether there were a few more minutes for sleep, or whether you should drag yourself from bed and grit your teeth against the cold.

Sam Carl knew the light—it was time to get out of bed.

He lifted the wool blanket and watched his tiny son breathe, saw those fat little lips moving in and out, plump belly rising and falling like dust from a bone-dry lake. And beside the boy, all bronze skin and naked to the waist, he saw his wife. Erin was turned away from the boy and Sam, her flank nudged against the boy's fat little arm—one year since his birth, and Reagan Hayes

Carl still clung to his mother like moss on a stone.

Sam didn't expect that to change. Not ever.

He lowered the blanket, bunched it beneath Erin's slim shoulder, and swung his feet to the carpet. Not too cold in the apartment, but he still shivered when his bare thighs touched the air. Fleeting pain hit his lower back and plunged down his left leg. He shifted his head and stood, a hand lodged on his right hip. The pain vanished. *I'm just stiff from work,* Sam thought, *that's all it is.* His knees ached, too. But that was normal, accrued interest from eight years as a short-order cook in a small-town diner. There were worse punishments for men. Much worse.

Sam slid each leg into his old sweatpants—gray with holes in the crotch—and shuffled into the kitchen. Without socks, the knife-pocked linoleum was cold against his feet. He turned once to see how the light fell across the used sofa and coffee table. It came through pink curtains Erin had found at a garage sale the previous summer, but Sam knew what kind of light it was—he guessed: *It's 5:48 in the morning.* When he turned to the digital readout on the stove, he chirped his lips in disappointment. The display churned from 6:01 to 6:02.

I was close. Fourteen minutes is pretty close.

He moved to the counter, touched a button on the coffeemaker, and waited for the familiar hiss of steam. A hiss that reminded him of dropping a lit match into cold white snow. The last time it'd snowed in the desert, a year ago to the month, Sam had done a thing he kept trying to forget, but it came back to him when steam bloomed from the coffeemaker's plastic lid.

It kept coming back to him, and he kept pushing it away— down a dark hole in his mind.

Like lowering a body into a grave.

Out the kitchen window, Sam studied the dirt yard where he was trying to level a place for a sandbox, a few square feet where his son could dig without running into rattlesnakes or scorpions. Plunged into the hard dirt, a shovel jutted at the sky like an old man's finger.

Oh, hell, Sam thought, *the holes we dig.*

Speaking of snow: He leaned over the sink and peered skyward. Low cloud cover blocked the sun, and Sam figured it was cold enough.

Today, he thought, *might be the day.*

A little snow sure would give Hayes Simms—Sam's closest buddy—something to bitch about. Hell, it'd give them both something to bitch about, and if that's what it took to fill the silence, so be it. Today was the first day Sam planned to see his best friend since Hayes—the small-town war hero—had gotten back from Afghanistan. He'd been home for a week or so, but Sam kept putting the damn meeting off, and it was Erin who'd made him promise to go this Sunday morning, the first of two days off from work at the diner.

More steam poured from the coffeemaker, and Sam leaned down to see the pot half full. He poured a cup and sank into a chair at a little wooden dining table, a thrift-store treasure. The coffee warmed him some, and he began to think about his friend.

You grow up and you think about the stupid things you did as a kid, the things you can't believe you got away with, even in a small town. Sam remembered when, in the seventh grade, they'd stolen an old Ford truck from behind the hardware store. It was a '69, one of those white trucks with a utility bed in back for tools. Hayes had found the keys under the front seat, and they'd hopped in like it was theirs. Sam never forgot how Hayes tried three times to start the thing before he figured out he needed to engage the clutch. Shit, they'd ridden dirt bikes, but never had a shot at the real deal. Turned out, Hayes taught himself to drive.

See, Sam told himself, *Ryder Simms—Hayes's father—had nothing to do with it.* Like Sam, Hayes didn't need his daddy, not for anything. When the Ford started, Hayes had screamed out the window, "Hell yes, Officer! We're on our way!"

Like the truck belonged to a deputy or something.

Sam was too chicken-shit to do any of the driving. That's how it always was with them: Hayes did the dirty work and Sam watched from wherever he felt safe.

Like with the war.

They took the Ford up Old Woman Springs Road—Hayes kept the thing screaming in second gear because he couldn't shift for shit—and found a long dirt road where the only thing that mattered was speed. Hayes had wrapped his fingers around the steering wheel and told Sam to hold on to his ass.

"What are you gonna do?"

"Shut up, Sam. Don't be a whiner—we're out for some thrills."

Sam didn't hold on to his ass, but he wrapped his fingers beneath the bench seat's bottom lip and prayed. Hayes floored it and the desert started to spin past them like a fast-forwarded film. Sam tried to count the Joshua trees for a moment, but the spiky limbs ran together like teeth beneath the purple splash of sunlight hitting thin clouds. Even the mountains, flushed against the distant blue, turned into one long line of horizon. That old engine held up for a good few miles. Dust flew out behind them, rose into the air and drifted across the desert. The floorboards rattled like an aftershock. Sam could still feel it, the way the floorboards had vibrated through his boot soles. The engine soared with a low, long note, screamed against its own metal and grease and heat. It reminded Sam of an old vacuum, but louder. Hayes had laughed the whole time, slapped the steering wheel like the kid he was. They hit a hill, and the truck bounced and slammed back against its suspension. That's when the engine gave up, dribbled out what little life it had left. White smoke poured from the hood, and Sam smelled burning coolant in the cabin. Hayes kept it floored and laughed harder, higher, longer. Sam never laughed when a good scream did better. That's what he did—he screamed. Soon, liquid exploded right against the windshield, looked like someone had thrown a clear egg at the thing. The Ford wouldn't go anymore, no matter how hard Hayes pumped the gas pedal and, at long last, they came to a stop. They got out and watched the white smoke pour from the engine. It hissed and groaned and cracked. That engine died about as slow as you might imagine, with little whimpers and a few last pleas for life. But an engine's got no say when it goes—they say life is a gift, and it is. "Good truck, that Ford," Hayes had said.

"Yes, it was."

That's not the worst of what they did, but it kind of represented the whole. What Sam remembered was that, for the most part, they were harmless. Just two kids trying to escape whatever it was that had them by the throat. Now, after Hayes had been twice to war and back, Sam thought it had to do with growing up where they did. Maybe it was some kind of infection, a thing that resisted all kinds of medicine. What did they call that? *A superbug*, he thought. They were troublemakers. So what? At the time, Sam never thought about what they'd become, what they'd do.

Erin coughed in the bedroom. Sam stood and poured her a cup of coffee. He set it on the table and sat down to wait. After a minute or so, she came in wearing pink fluffy socks, blue pajama pants, and a gray hooded sweater. "Hey, early riser." She rubbed her eyes and sat across from him.

"I made it strong today." He lifted his mug at her, mimed a toast.

Erin sipped, rolled the liquid in her mouth, and shrugged. "I bet I could make it stronger." She yawned, set the mug down and lifted her arms in a childlike stretch. "When are you heading up to see Hayes?"

"I was thinking about it, Erin. I'm not sure I'm ready for that. I'm not sure I'm ready to..." He didn't know how to say that he was afraid. He clamped his mouth shut.

Erin lowered her outstretched arms and pinned him with a blue-eyed stare. "Sam, you need to go see the man. He's been home for over a week and he's living up there alone. He's wondering—I bet he's wondering—where the hell you've been. His best friend. The only thing he's got." She lifted her mug and sipped without averting her stare.

"Maybe he wants to be alone."

"It doesn't matter what he wants. What matters is what he needs."

"How do you know what he needs?"

Erin cocked her head. A slight smile twitched from one corner of her mouth. "Sam, I'm an expert in the ways of men. That's why I have you wrapped around my little pinkie finger. Hayes needs his buddy to go up there and say hello, let him know that he's welcome and that he's got a pal when he needs it. It's not algebra, and it's sure as hell not calculus."

"Like you know either."

"I know you're the missing variable right this minute."

Sam chuckled and winked at his wife. "Clever."

"Well, I'm good for something. Didn't I tell you that from the beginning?" Erin stood and moved toward him. She clutched his face with both hands and pulled his head to her stomach. "I bet you didn't even think I was good for you."

Sam pushed his forehead into her, remembered doing the same thing while she was pregnant and feeling the subtle kicks and feints of his unborn son. "I knew I was good for you. And that you were right for me."

"But not good?"

"Good and right are pretty close, Erin."

"I suppose they're close, but they're not the same." She laughed and played her fingers along his chin. She rubbed the thin purple scar that ran along the left side of Sam's face.

There it was, the scar to remind him of Ryder Simms.

Always, there was the scar. And the thing from last year. That, too, was part of the scar—it flowed from the scar, burst from it like a cactus plume. "I'll miss you today," Sam said.

Erin rubbed her thumb along the raised ridge of skin. "How's your back feel today? Did you get those insoles like I told you?"

"It's okay. I feel it, but I can tell it's better. Getting better."

"And the insoles?"

"They're in my boots, sweetie."

"You know I'm going to check."

"You don't trust me, lady?" Sam smiled, anticipating Erin's reply.

She didn't disappoint. "Oh, Sam—I trust you. I just don't believe I should."

"There it is again, that clever wordplay."

"And you're going to run over to the diner and get your paycheck, right? I want to deposit it tomorrow morning. That way, we can have some money in the bank for groceries on Tuesday."

"You want me to deposit it?"

Erin pulled her hands away from his face and slid them onto his shoulder blades. "Last time, you forgot, and I like to make sure we don't forget."

Sam spoke into her stomach. "I'll get my check. Don't worry."

"And don't think you're rich either."

"No kidding. Believe me, I'm under no delusions."

Erin laughed and moved back to her chair, sat with one foot tucked beneath her. "You mean illusions, Sam."

"No, I mean delusions."

"That's what you think you mean." She lifted her mug and sipped the coffee. Her eyes drilled into him, pinned him in the morning air. "You need to start meaning what *I* think you should mean."

"Oh, is that right?"

"You bet."

2

You get to know a place well enough, and it becomes the only thing you know.

You become part of the landscape, and then comes the reverse—the place knows you better than you know yourself. That's how Sam felt about the desert. He'd lived in the same town his whole life, and he knew how that must seem to people from the outside, or to people who left and came back to the place. It made him look simple. And it made him look foolish. But Sam didn't see himself like that. Instead, he saw a person who stuck with what he understood, what he could fathom on a day-to-day basis.

And if those things made him weak or a coward, well, he was weak. And he was a coward. But he was not simple. And he was not, in the standard sense of the word, foolish. As Sam closed the apartment door behind him and walked toward his old Chevy truck, he glanced at the nearby foothills. Gray clouds now hung low and thick, and Sam did not see blue sky in the day's future. Gangly Joshua trees stood out in the distance, and the hills flushed jagged against the receding night. He unlocked the Chevy and hopped into the driver's seat. He pumped the gas pedal and waited for a moment. An old truck needed love to start in weather like this. He flipped the key, and the engine rattled, staggered, burned to life with a throaty wheeze. Sam strapped the seat belt across his body, shifted the truck into reverse, and checked his mirrors. Behind him, the dirt driveway fed onto a rain-rutted dirt road. Beyond that, creosote and yucca plants dotted flatland running backward into distant foothills.

Yes, Sam thought, this landscape knew him as well as he knew it.

So, what did the desert know about Sam Carl?

He was twenty-six years old and a high school graduate. He was married to his high school sweetheart, and they had a little boy together. He was a short-order cook in a greasy-spoon diner, and he was three months behind on his electric bill. He could still throw a decent curveball and fit into Levi's from his senior year. Sam had nine silver fillings in his mouth and a case of athlete's foot he couldn't shake. He drove a Chevy truck with 164,000 miles on a rebuilt V-8.

All these were things that other people knew. This was stuff anybody could see, if they wanted to look.

What people didn't know, and what they couldn't see, was that other thing, a thing the desert knew all too well: Yes, the Sam Carl who worked the grill at the diner, the one with the wife and kid, the one who was once—maybe still—best friends with the war hero, *that* Sam Carl was something far more. He was, the desert knew, a cold-blooded killer.

Before Everything

Desert shrub poked at Sam's cheeks as he lifted his head from the sandy desert floor. The shrub's pungent scent—peppery, thick, part-sweet—tickled his throat, thickened the saliva in his mouth. Through the brush, Sam watched Hayes Simms—even then, his best and closest friend—stroll between scattered cholla and knee-high boulders, a stringy-haired ten-year-old soldier stalking his prey.

In the still afternoon air, Hayes stopped, scanned the desert. His eyes stopped without recognition above Sam's hiding spot. Sam caught his breath as fear built in his chest, a knotted tension between his ribs. Hayes shifted a rifle-length two-by-four from one shoulder to the other. Sam still lay sprawled in the dirt like an iguana. Beside him was his own two-by-four—these harmless pieces of lumber were their guns.

When he didn't catch any movement, Hayes turned his back to Sam, placed a flat hand over his eyes to see into the sunlight. Sam took the chance to stand, press his gun to his chest, and sprint twenty yards to a large boulder. He kneeled in the dirt, rested there with his back against the cool, hard granite and tried to quell the birds flapping around in his belly. Why was he nervous? They were pointing two-by-fours at each other and yelling "you got shot, sucker!" But when Sam played war games with Hayes, an odd uncertainty filled his head—he felt like maybe they had real guns with real bullets, like maybe Hayes wanted to kill him for real, like maybe he shouldn't win the game or Hayes might... What? Phantom punches from Hayes's fists dug into Sam's skinny belly. In his mind, Sam saw the familiar outline of anger etched on his friend's face, like when Hayes heard his father's voice or when a teacher called to him with that sing-song taunt of authority. Sam knew the guns and bullets and fists weren't real, but that didn't stop his chest from screaming with tension, his breath coming short and hard, his belly flopping like a flimsy pancake.

To his left, a few yards away, Sam heard the light crunch of boot sole against dirt—it came twice, stopped for thirty seconds. Then it came again.

He thought to circle the boulder, press in on Hayes and lift the two-by-four at him with a loud, wild screech—Sam could not think of a time when he had scared Hayes. Not once had he made his best friend jump, howl, or look at him with the bright, tiny kid eyes Sam saw in their friends at school. It was like Hayes expected everything that came at him. Or for him.

Still, Sam convinced himself: *One day, I'm going to scare the bastard.*

Not now, though. Not today.

The crunch of boot sole came to him again, and Sam moved away from it, pivoted against the boulder in the opposite direction. The safest thing? Let Hayes wander past, ramble through the desert until he grew tired and dusk fell like a blindness. The alternative was—as Sam's dad called it—hand-to-hand combat. Whether or not Sam got the drop on him, Hayes would insist

Sam's gun misfired or that his aim was shoddy, and the two boys would fall to wrestling in the dirt. Last time they'd done this, Sam had found himself with dirt in his eyes and warm trickles of blood on his elbows. Yes, they were messing around, but it still hurt to fight with Hayes.

I'll hide from him, Sam thought. *I'll sneak around and keep cover, watch while he tries to spot my shadow and swings his gun on fleeing jackrabbits.*

The scabs from last time were still rough on Sam's elbows—he didn't want to fight Hayes again. Somehow, the other boy made him feel small, though they were the same age and height. And it wasn't that Sam couldn't hold his own with Hayes. Sam was just as likely to flip Hayes onto his back or shove his face into the dirt as the other way around. When Sam looked at it pound for pound, he and Hayes were much the same, but he still felt small around his friend.

Another crunch. A scrape. The predatory creak of the two-by-four shifting positions. And after those sounds, Hayes whispered to the desert, "Where the hell are you, Sam? This ain't hide-and-seek."

Sam held his breath. He stood slowly, crept away from the whisper. Sam knew how to keep quiet, how to move like an animal. This from too many nights in the trailer while his parents shouted curses at each other beneath the desert's velvet moonlight. They took it outside when they fought. He often awoke to half shouts, slurred insults, and—twice, he remembered—the dull and frightening thud of his father's fists. It was on those nights, when he heard the shouts, that Sam left his bed, tiptoed into the trailer's living area, and grabbed a handful of jelly beans from a jar near the sink. He'd lie in bed—not crying, not ever—and listen to their shouts while his tiny, shaking hands fed one bright jelly bean after another through his lips.

As he crept away from Hayes, Sam gulped air and tried not to scrape his boots in the dirt. He moved when he sensed Hayes moving. He breathed when he sensed Hayes breathing. *I'm a shadow,* Sam thought. *I'm a shadow as dark as pond water.* He rounded the large boulder, leaned into its cool surface, and saw Hayes appear before him in scuffed boots and blackened Levi's. He wore a loose-fitting gray T-shirt with holes showing along its bottom. Hayes took two more steps and lifted a hand to his forehead. His two-by-four rested on one shoulder, harmless as an umbrella. Sam grinned. All at once, his fear vanished. The flutters in his stomach subsided—he saw only the gray target of Hayes's backside, his T-shirt rustling in the intermittent desert breeze. *I've got a clear shot,* Sam thought. *I'm going to scare the shit out of Hayes.*

I'm going to make the bastard jump.

Sam lifted his two-by-four, pointed it like a rifle.

He pursed his lips and took a deep breath.

3

At the main road, Sam looked both ways—west toward a long stretch that led to cities, government offices, civilization; then east toward the small town and the bleached desert beyond, sprawling like a tongue. He steered the Chevy east. On the radio, a country singer rattled on about losing his wife in a snowstorm, about hearing her cries through his cabin's cedar walls. But it was a whiteout, and the man couldn't see a thing—he listened to her die, cold and afraid.

The road was nearly vacant. A few cars, their headlights dim against the morning gray, moved at Sam from the distance. The road lay flat in the valley and angled crosswise into town. It flooded in places if and when it rained. Sam dreaded the spring when the sudden storms made it possible to be cut off from town or work or a good drink at a bar. And now that Reagan was born, Sam worried about being cut off from his son, stuck at work while Erin tried to keep the wood-burning stove hot. Funny, the way he'd started to worry once Erin got pregnant. About money. About storms. About life and death. About everything. When these worries came to the front of his mind, Sam sometimes felt his heart quicken, his throat begin to close—he had trouble breathing and holding himself upright.

He gripped the steering wheel tighter, told himself to relax. The money, he could think about the money. It was a problem, a constant challenge, but it was a challenge with which he coped.

And today was payday, a few hours of hard-earned relief.

He'd get his paycheck and head up to see Hayes. *Maybe*, he thought, *I'll spend a couple hours with the guy, but that's it.* It wasn't that Sam didn't want to see Hayes. It was that he wanted to see the Hayes he knew, the old Hayes who didn't go fight some war in a place Sam couldn't point to on an unlabeled map. The first time Hayes came back, after nine months in Afghanistan, he'd been aloof, sort of half-awake while Sam dragged him through town. Sam decided, after three days, they just didn't have much to talk about. Funny, because it used to be that talking was the farthest thing from necessary—they'd spent lots of time together in silence.

Never, not once, did that matter.

But when Hayes came back, it was awkward to be around the man. Silence and brooding looks. Plus, there was something else: Sam kept hearing this voice inside him, a whisper that said it should be him over there, and not Hayes. He kept telling himself the voice was the stupid inside him. But it was still there. Maybe he should be the one over there carrying a gun and eating vacuum-packed food. Or, hell, he should at least be over there with Hayes, not back here flipping burgers and watching Cartoon Network before bed. That feeling, Sam thought it might be the beginning of shame. It wasn't guilt or a partly veiled triumph, like with the other thing lurking in the dark parts of his mind.

No, it *was* shame.

He slowed as he came over a rise and let the Chevy glide past a series of small shops and offices. You had your real estate folks, your lawyer (a couple, actually), your dentists, and a few antique shops with "closed" signs in their windows. Same old small-town business association. Sam slowed as John's Place, the diner, emerged from the gray backdrop of sky. He pulled into the lot, but there were no cars. Sundays the place opened late—eight in the morning. Sam figured Nelson, his boss, should be in by seven, but it didn't look like that was going to happen. For a moment, Sam studied the low-slung building and the pink neon sign along its top. The windows were still dark, flecked with dust at their edges, and a Styrofoam cup rolled back and forth near the front door. *How much of your life can you spend here? All of it? How much of your life* will *you spend here? You better start doing some big-time thinking, buddy. If not, you're going to wind up a fat old man in an apron—is that what you want?*

Sam shook his head and grunted. He pulled the Chevy through the parking lot, bumped onto the road and accelerated eastward.

He hooked a right on Juniper, pushed the truck onto a slow-rising grade. Four stop signs to the elementary school, he knew. Four four-way stops until you get to school. He smiled to himself. *God, what I wouldn't give to go back there.* Before the shouting matches between his parents—and before his father left—Sam looked back on his childhood as a time without worry. His purpose was simple: go to school, play, and go home. A kid's job... to have fun. He wished he'd known that you never have that again. It vanishes as soon as you hit eighteen. Earlier for Sam. Things are expected of you after that.

When he reached the school, Sam again pulled the Chevy into the parking lot. He knocked the transmission into park and sat there with the engine pushing heat into the cab. He switched off the radio, annoyed with an auto-tuned country singer screeching on about beer and baseball. The school building was surrounded by low chain-link fencing painted blue. Oh, to walk through those gates again and start over, that would be something: Nearly twenty years ago Sam was going to this school—a maze of thin-walled buildings he remembered as much larger—with a future war hero. Back then, it seemed they could do whatever the hell they wanted: Astronaut? Sure. Policeman? Easy as a dropkick. Professional baseball player? If you work hard enough. *No,* Sam thought, *not true at all.* He shook his head. You don't know. You just never know. Sometimes, for some people, it all goes to hell.

There are signs, clues to what a person will become, how they'll live.

Sam looked back and, now that he was older, saw those signs in Hayes. One day in third grade, their teacher, Mr. Burks—his glasses tilted and his hair in a thin comb-over—gave Hayes a gunslinger's look. With his scuffed cowboy boots and loose Levi's down on his hips, Mr. Burks always stomped around the class like a small-town sheriff. "Mr. Simms," he said, "I want to know what in the heck you think you're doing to that desk."

Hayes looked up from his desk, where he'd etched the word *jerk* into the wood with a pocketknife, and smiled with the gapped teeth of a nine-year-old boy. He told Sam he didn't know why he'd done it, but it somehow felt good to use the knife's sharp point to scratch hard lines into the desk. The word had a nice round sound to it, like a curse word without all the fuss. "I'm not doing nothing, sir," Hayes had said.

Obscured by the desk, Hayes folded the pocketknife closed and, with his right hand, held it out to Sam sitting at the desk beside him. Mr. Burks couldn't see this exchange, though he could see the boy's shoulder move slightly, as if he were using a stick to draw a circle into sand. A few children giggled. Mr. Burks ambled through desks and stopped in front of Hayes. Hayes shuffled his feet and took a deep, dramatic breath. For kids like Hayes and Sam, there was trouble and there was punishment. The two were separate, but at certain moments, they might come together—this was one of those moments. Hayes brought his hands out from beneath the desk and rested them palms down on the wood surface. He tried to cover the etched word with one hand, his fingers curled slightly toward his chest.

Mr. Burks groaned, used a piece of chalk to sketch a thin white line around Hayes's hand. When he finished the odd-shaped drawing, he said, "Go ahead and lift up. We want to see the crime scene, Mr. Simms."

Hayes lifted his hand and dropped it into his lap. The teacher stared at the word for quite some time. He tore his eyes away and studied each of the nearby children. There was silence in the room, an ominous darkness of sound that made Sam uneasy.

Mr. Burks held his hand out, palm up, and said, "Give it to me."

"What?"

"Whatever you scratched the desk with—I want it."

Hayes folded his lips downward and set his gaze against the old-man teacher. Next to him, Sam stared straight ahead, tried not to give away that he had the knife. Hayes said, "I'll never give you what you want."

Mr. Burks sighed with impatience and said, "Mr. Simms has scratched a word into his desk, everybody. What do we call that here in school?"

A little girl up front shouted, "We call it defacing property!"

"That's right, Cheryl. Mr. Simms here has defaced school property. Why don't you read your word aloud, Mr. Simms? Tell us what you wrote."

Hayes looked at the desk, at the word scratched into the ribbed wood, and smiled. After a second, he said, "I wrote the word *fuck*. And I'm sorry I wrote that word."

The class laughed together.

Blood rushed into the teacher's pasty cheeks, colored him from his chin to his neck. "That's not the word, Mr. Simms, and you know it." The class quieted and Sam's laughter outlasted them. His childish squeal faded like wind into a dark tunnel. Mr. Burks said, "What did you write?"

"You're right. *Fuck* wasn't it. I wrote *jerk*."

"Get up, Mr. Simms."

Hayes stood, shoved his hands into his pockets. He stooped slightly, an old-man child too tired to straighten. "Sorry about that, Mr. Burks."

"At least I know you can read."

"And spell."

More laughter from the class. Sam bit his bottom lip, tried not to laugh too hard. The commotion was met with another gunslinger's stare from Mr. Burks. He shook his head slowly at Hayes, studied him like he would a cell through a microscope. "I don't understand you, Hayes. You know what that word means to you right this second?"

Hayes nodded and said, "It means detention."

"You got it. Go on."

Hayes moved past the teacher, walked down the long row of desks, and pushed out the classroom door into the open-air hallway. Behind him, Mr. Burks stood frozen, his big adult eyes locked on the jagged word etched into the wooden desk.

Sam had never given that pocketknife back to Hayes. He'd kept it until adulthood and still carried it on his keychain. He never understood why Hayes got himself in trouble—it was all avoidable. Being a kid to Sam meant finding a way to get away with things. The only trouble was whether adults found out about it. Hayes, it seemed to Sam, wanted to get into trouble, and he wanted to be punished. It was like fuel for Hayes, a thing he needed to certify his own existence. The attention it brought put Hayes in front of the world, put him out where his classmates and teachers would see him for what he was, or for what he wanted them to think he was. It made Sam uncomfortable to think about his closest friend that way, but he'd stopped kidding himself about it as they grew. You have a friend who does bad things, and you start to see that friend as a bad thing himself. Yet another thing you push to a place you can't see. There are things you can do about it, Sam knew—you can leave a person alone, up and forget about your friendship, your brotherhood. You can try to change a person or make them see it another way, from a backward sight according to them. But does any of that work? Not with Hayes it didn't.

And Sam couldn't say Hayes was a bad person—he wasn't bad.

No, he was dark and lost and forgotten, but he wasn't bad.

Sam looked at that pocketknife—it was rust red and dull as a slice of bread—when he found himself thinking of Hayes. It was a harmless weapon, and the word carved into that desk was harmless, too. But the act, Sam knew, was the real problem. It wasn't always the result that mattered, but the acts leading to the result, the careful considerations of those acts and their intended damage. Forget about the damage, the world said, and look at what leads to the damage. It seemed all backward to Sam, to see the end as a nothing, and the events that led to that end a whole series of bad somethings. His mind tripped over this idea like it stumbled over Hayes and all the things he did, where they did and didn't lead.

To today, Sam thought. *All the way to today.* He wiped sweat from his forehead. The heater in the Chevy worked for its money, that was for sure. Sam knew by the light—there's that light again—that it was near eight, 7:42 by his guess, and Nelson should be at the diner. If not, he was already behind. *I hope he is. I'll laugh my ass off, and he'll take it as I give it.* Sam shifted into drive, flipped a lazy U-turn, and headed back through the four four-way stops.

It was time to get paid.

When Sam walked into John's Place, Nelson was at the flat-top grill cooking a sheet of bacon. He stood there with a steel spatula, his grease-stained apron dangling from his neck. His hair was mussed, and his Levi's hung low across his ass. The old man turned to Sam and shook his head. "You can't even deposit a paycheck on Sunday, Sam. Why the hell do you insist on coming in for the dang thing?"

Sam propped himself on one of the stools at the diner. He watched the bacon sizzle and opened and squeezed his right fist. With the tips of his fingers, Sam felt the skin on that palm. It was scarred, a mangled landscape of nerve endings and ridges. A memory began to surface, but Sam pushed it away, shoved it beneath black waters in his mind. *That's all you do*, he told himself, *push memories from your head.* He placed his hands flat against the counter, pulled his gaze from the bacon, and let himself forget. "If you let us do direct deposit I wouldn't have to pick anything up, now would I?"

Nelson shrugged. "You know I'm set in my ways, Sam."

"Like the rest of us."

The old cook turned to Sam, raised his eyebrows, and whistled for a short moment. "You're up early, though. Usually, I don't see you until noon, when I have to fight through the lunch rush and find your damn check. What you up to today?"

"I'm supposed to go see Hayes."

"Is that right? You tell that boy to get on down here. His next meal is on me." Nelson pointed at Sam with the spatula. "You, though, you always have to pay."

Sam ignored the comment and said, "Can I have my paycheck now, or do I have to fight you for it?"

Nelson turned to the grill. In one smooth motion, he slipped the long steel spatula beneath a row of curled bacon, scooped upward, twisted, and set the strips down on their opposite sides. He rested the spatula on the grill and said, "Watch the bacon, Sam. I'll be back in a second."

Sam walked around the counter and hovered near the grill. The pungent smell of animal fat filled his nostrils, made his stomach churn. He grabbed the spatula, scooped up a piece and, with his left hand, pinched it between thumb and forefinger. He blew on the bacon and shoved it through his lips. While he chewed with an open mouth, Sam saw a red Chevy—a hell of a lot newer and nicer than his own—turn left across the street and pull into the parking lot. It swiveled into a spot, the brake lights flashed red, and Jazz, the local Marine Corps recruiter, opened the driver's side door and stepped onto the pavement. The last of the bacon slipped down Sam's throat. Heat ran down into his belly and warmed him to the core.

Last he'd seen Jazz was a few months prior, before Sam knew Hayes was on his way home. They'd had drinks at a little saloon down the street. He hadn't expected to see Jazz today. It made Sam uneasy, seeing Jazz on the same day he was supposed to see Hayes. *Why? Why should it?*

Because, he reminded himself, *Hayes does not like this son of a gun. He never did, and you know that from the tip of your nose all the way down to your toes.* Sam watched as Jazz adjusted his tan uniform shirt, latched a hand to his belt and tightened it. Jazz reached back into the truck and pulled out a heavy black coat, shrugged it over his shoulders and shivered into it. Jazz was older now, like Sam and Hayes, but he looked and carried himself the same—not a wrinkle on his smooth, white face.

One morning a few weeks before they'd graduated high school, while they sat in this very same diner, Hayes had told Sam he'd hated Jazz from the moment he saw him. He knew it before he heard the man speak. It got to Hayes, the way Jazz's shiny, clean-shaven jaw worked while he spoke or chewed a stack of pancakes, how the muscles pulsed in the man's cheeks like fists.

And when Jazz ate breakfast in John's Place, he ate like he owned the world. He draped his elbows across the counter and spread his legs across two stools. Sam remembered watching from across their booth as Hayes pressed his lips together and stared at the son of a gun. Bacon grease and hash potato smells soaked the air. Beneath that, the acrid tinge of burning coffee. Hayes had snorted and tried to catch the eyes of a little, round waitress who pranced across the diner. She'd ignored him. He drummed his fingers on the table. Sam did not flag the waitress. She'd come when she was ready. Instead, he watched as Hayes settled his eyes back on the man sitting at the countertop. Sam turned to take in the scene: Jazz wore his United States Marine uniform—red stripe running down blue slacks with a crisp, tan shirt and hat perched on a bouncing knee. Those fists in his cheeks kept moving, in and out, like a heartbeat. Sweat glistened on his forehead. He dabbed at his mouth with a crumpled white napkin, tossed it onto the counter, and started again with his chewing.

Did Hayes see another man while he watched the Marine? Sam wondered if Hayes saw his own father, Ryder Simms, the old man with stringy white hair and a voice that rattled like rocks in a tin can. Maybe he saw those same muscles pulsing in his father's cheeks, a tough piece of rabbit meat mashing between his lips. Hayes had told Sam about how he'd gone hunting with his father the summer prior, how they'd humped it four miles into the foothills, carried jugs of water at their hips and a gun each; Hayes with a pistol, an old Luger, and Ryder Simms with a shotgun hanging from a shoulder strap. You didn't hunt in the dead heat of summer, Sam knew, unless you were Ryder Simms. Then, you did whatever you wanted, whatever you felt needed doing, and however you felt you needed to do it.

Sam tried to catch his buddy's eyes, but Hayes was fixated on Jazz, watching him with odd determination.

The waitress—without asking—brought Hayes and Sam cups of black coffee. "You know what you want? Same as always, or you gonna switch?" She wiped sweat from her cheeks with the back of one hand. It was September and the diner was hot, summer's tail end making the desert sweat to death.

Without taking his eyes from the Marine, Hayes said, "Two eggs, over easy. I want a English muffin. Burn it to hell. And raspberry jam. That's my favorite."

Sam nodded and smiled at the waitress. "Coffee and an egg sandwich, add tomato."

"What I thought, same as always." She backed away, disappeared.

Sam lifted the coffee mug to his lips. It went down like tar. Bottom of the pot, like usual. He took another sip. And another. What was it that put this thing in Hayes, his tendency to hate? Sam saw flashes of it their entire lives, but it thickened as they got older, like a scent you couldn't rub off your skin.

For Sam, Jazz did somehow conjure inward echoes of Ryder. Vague notions of fear and uncertainty, a ball-dropping darkness that made Sam clench his stomach muscles. It wasn't the creases in Jazz's pants and shirt. Or the hat. Perhaps it was how the Marine moved, how he chewed and breathed and sat, that sketched him like Ryder Simms. Except the Marine wasn't Ryder Simms. How could he be? This man—whatever Hayes and Sam felt or dared to think—had a life going for himself. He drove a pickup truck and took home a paycheck. And they often saw Jazz with women at the movie theater, young almost-women is what they were, but still, it was true.

Not like Ryder, who was a beast unto himself.

All Sam could fathom was that the world was a place of indefinite lines, a place of fog and half-phantoms.

Sam let this go for a moment and turned his view to the window. It looked out on the two-lane roadway and the trailer park a few hundred yards south. Beyond that, saw-blade hills bit purple-rinsed sky. The sun lifted from the east, burned round like the tip of a cigarette. Sam angled his lanky frame across the booth and turned back to Hayes. His dark eyebrows dipped, raised into an arch. "What the hell are you staring at, Hayes?"

"Jarhead." It came out loud—everybody in the place heard it, even over the sound of steel spatulas tapping against the sizzling flat-top grill. John's Place had one of those open kitchens, where you could watch and make sure the cook wasn't sweating into your eggs. "Damn jarhead," Hayes said.

Sam knew Jazz heard, that it pissed the guy off, at the very least. He turned around, caught sight of Jazz shoving a triple-decker triangle of pancakes into his mouth. He turned back toward Hayes, rapped his knuckle against the table. "Leave the guy alone, Hayes. He's not doing anything."

"What for?"

"He's eating his breakfast. Not bothering us."

"He's bothering me. I don't like his uniform. The way he chews, I don't like that."

"Shit, man. What do you have against them?"

Hayes swung his eyes to Sam, ran his tongue over his bottom lip and tilted his head to one side. "Everything I can. My question is, what don't I have against them? Shit, why don't you have anything against them?"

"You know why."

"Still thinking about joining up, huh?"

"Go to hell." Sam rubbed his neck. He grunted at Hayes. "You're a damn bastard. No good is what you are." Sam *was* thinking about joining the Marine Corps, but fear held him back from signing the papers. Shit, fear held him back from talking to Jazz. He wanted to be tough and mean, but he didn't understand how to push himself into that world. Hayes didn't have that trouble. It started with Ryder, and Hayes kept it up with the rest of the world. The way Hayes saw it, you needed to fight your parents first, and then you could fight everybody else.

Diner sounds penetrated Sam's thoughts. The tinkle of forks on porcelain, muffled conversations, and the low growl of the Marine's voice as he talked to the waitress.

Hayes squinted and tried to make out the words. "You know I'm kidding," he said to Sam, "that I'm messing with you."

"No," Sam said, "I know you're not."

Hayes shrugged, watched the waitress high-step toward them. She poured fresh coffee into the mug beneath Sam's chin. "It's all free today. Your breakfast is taken care of."

Hayes said, "To hell with that. I don't take anything free."

"Free breakfast? I don't mind."

"We don't take it for free. Nothing's free in this life."

"Sometimes breakfast is," Sam said.

The waitress scampered behind the counter.

Hayes twisted his bottom lip beneath the top row of his teeth, bit into skin. "No, it ain't. Not ever."

The waitress came back with two white plates, dropped them on the table and vanished. "Looks good." Hayes piled jam onto his English muffin and tore into it like a dog. He chewed with an open mouth, drained coffee between bites.

"You eat like an animal."

Hayes shoved more muffin into his mouth, chewed. After a moment, he leaned back and tilted his eyes at the ceiling. He dropped the butter knife on the table.

Sam caught a floral scent—cologne, real cologne—as it drifted across the table, overpowered the grease and cooked meat. Jazz stood over them. He held his billed hat with both hands at his waist. His face was clean-shaven and his eyes were the big kind, round and blue and way more excited than they should be. He cleared his throat and stared at the center of the table. Not at Sam or Hayes, but at the table where the salt and pepper shakers sat.

Sam put his sandwich down and waited.

Jazz cleared his throat again, grunted. "I figure, a man of my status can buy you boys some breakfast, can't he?"

"Nope. He can't," Hayes said.

"You're too good for my hard-earned money. I can see that, the way you cinch those jeans tight with that belt. And that white T-shirt, too. You're too classy for a free breakfast. I can see that."

"From you, we are."

"I appreciate the offer," Sam said.

"No, he doesn't," Hayes countered. He hit Sam with fiery eyes for a second, looked back at Jazz. "I don't like you, and I don't like what you do." It spilled out with a sneer.

"What is it you think I do?"

"Lie to poor kids. That's what."

"I never lied in my life."

"Shit," Hayes said, and picked up his fork. He scooped a forkful of eggs over his lips and chewed with his mouth open, clicked his teeth together.

"A kid like you, you're what? Eighteen, maybe? Or just about. A kid like you"—Jazz settled his eyes on Hayes—"would make one hell of a Marine. You just let me know when you get interested and we'll talk about it." He dipped two fingers into a breast pocket and threw a white business card onto the table between the white plates. "There's my number. Enjoy your breakfast, boys."

Sam turned in the booth and, along with Hayes, watched the Marine walk out and nod at everybody with that billed cap in his hands. The glass front door jingled a little bell and the conversations in the diner started again. Hayes scooped some eggs into his mouth and grinned. "I bet that pissed him off. You think it was too much?"

But if it was too much, it still wasn't enough for Hayes.

Sam remembered how Hayes had dropped his fork, stalked through the diner, and confronted Jazz in the parking lot—it surprised him how Hayes stood talking to Jazz: His hands dangled from the pockets of his Levi's, and he wore an ill-fitting grin on his face. He ran a hand along the bed of Jazz's red pickup truck. But something odd happened as Sam watched. He saw Hayes move toward the Marine, lift his booted foot as if to strike him. But the Marine sidestepped, lunged, struck like a rattlesnake. His right arm looped Hayes's neck, gripped him beneath his chin. His shoulder muscles rippled through the tan shirt as he squeezed Hayes into submission.

Sam began to slide from the booth, but an old man a few chairs down said, "I'd leave the two of them alone, son." Sam watched through the window as Hayes kicked at hot air, wriggled his shoulders and, after the longest minute in Sam's life, dropped flat against the pavement. Jazz kneeled, set Hayes down gently, like a man laying out a blanket for a woman. He stood, pulled another business card from his pocket, and dropped it. It fluttered and spun like a falling leaf before landing on Hayes. His chest lifted and fell—a regular rhythm with the Marine's business card along for the ride. Jazz shook his head, glanced at the diner. He smirked before he climbed into the pickup and sped onto the highway.

Sam would always remember how Hayes looked when he regained consciousness—there was a vicious glare in his eyes, like a dog gets when a rabbit hops through dusk, a predatory glare before a frantic, bloody pursuit. The look never left Hayes after that. It lingered with him like regret, a faint tinge in his mannerisms and facial expressions. He wouldn't speak of that day, and Sam didn't ask about it. Sam knew Hayes changed on that summer morning.

And now, on the morning Sam was to see his best friend after a year at war, Jazz—all nonchalant, with fragile cheeks—sauntered into John's Place with a fat grin on his face. "Yo, Sam, how you doing, pal? It's cold out there."

Sam lifted his chin slightly, eyed the bacon again. He slid the spatula beneath the sizzling meat and scooped a few strips onto a mesh screen beside the grill. "I'm fine, just picking up my paycheck. How you doing, Jazz?"

Jazz—just like he used to do—set up camp at the diner counter, draped himself across two spaces. "Quick breakfast and I'm making a few house calls."

"Working on a Sunday, huh?" Sam lifted another row of bacon, dumped it onto the screen. "I thought you make your own schedule."

"That's the thing. I do. But half the time, nobody's home. What I do is hit the white trash in the morning—they don't go to church—and I hit the decent folks after church. Thing is, on

Sunday you get Mom and Dad at home. It's not just lip service from the kid." Jazz sniffed hard through his nose, bunched the coat around his neck. "It's even cold in here, man. You have a heater, what the hell?"

"It's Nelson," Sam said. "He doesn't want—"

"My bills to skyrocket. That's what." Nelson flapped an envelope in the air as he entered the kitchen area. "Otherwise, I can't pay this guy." He handed the envelope to Sam and waved him away. "Out of here, Sam. I don't want you billing me for five extra minutes on a Sunday."

Sam walked around the counter, gave Jazz a wide berth, and moved toward the door. "That's five minutes of overtime you owe me."

Nelson shook his head and chuckled.

Jazz turned and caught Sam's eye before he exited. "Hey, you ever hear from Hayes? He come back yet?"

Sam stopped, thought about lying, but decided against it. *I've got no reason to be uneasy—Jazz will find out about Hayes sooner or later.* "He's back. I'm headed up to see him today, this morning."

"No kidding?"

"Yeah, been back a week or so."

Jazz squinted and nodded with a measured expression. "You tell him I said hello, Sam. Maybe we'll run into each other around town."

"Maybe," Sam said. "I'll be seeing you." He turned to the door and pushed through it. The cold desert air smacked him in the face.

Sam heard Nelson's voice from inside the diner, "Don't let the door smack you on your way out..."

Before Everything

The peppery, part-sweet scent of desert shrub flowed across Sam's tongue, lodged at the back of his throat. There was a tickle, a scratch—*no*, Sam thought, *not now.*

Please, please don't let me cough.
Not while I have Hayes clear in my sights.

The cough in Sam's throat caught like a gnat, hung between his tongue and chest. While he moved backward, away from Hayes, a low roar came from the dirt road beyond the tract of desert where they stalked each other with the two-by-fours. They were walking distance from Sam's trailer—the boxy structure's blue awning visible above a rise dotted with wispy creosote bushes—and the road between was mostly vacant. It ran from the lower portion of the desert, through rocky foothills, and into a higher-elevation area where Hayes lived with his father. In fact, it was Ryder Simms who often used the road to either drop Hayes at Sam's or to pick him up late in the evenings. Last time he'd left Hayes, two days prior, Ryder hadn't returned for his boy, and Sam's mother let Hayes stay. What else could she do? Ryder didn't have a phone, and the boys ran and played together all day. They kept each other busy.

And now, as Ryder's white pickup truck rumbled down the road, a cloud of dust lifting from beneath the tires, Hayes lowered his two-by-four and bent to his knees. He ducked down and watched the truck approach. Sam waited behind him. He huddled next to the cold granite, pressed the nagging urge to cough back into his belly. The old truck's transmission squealed and ground at itself like a pepper mill, caught gear and churned toward the boys.

The truck stopped between them and Sam's trailer. Banjo music spilled from the radio, and the truck sputtered as it idled. Ryder leaned across the cab, and Sam watched as he squinted in their direction. *No way he can see us*, Sam thought, *not with his eyesight.* Ryder spit out the truck's open passenger window and yelled, "Hayes! You come on out! I ain't going to wait for you!"

Neither Hayes nor Sam answered.

Beyond the truck, the trailer door opened, and Sam's mother appeared. She waddled forward, stood with her hands on her hips as Ryder's truck idled like a monster. After contemplating, she said, "You trying for Hayes?"

Ryder yelled back, "Where in the hell is he?"

"They been gone a few hours."

Ryder's dead-glaze eyes swung back toward Hayes and Sam.

To himself, Hayes said, "I'll walk home when I'm ready."

"Hayes! Dammit, you get your ass over here or I'm gone!"

Sam watched as Hayes sat back in the dirt, crossed his legs, and ran his fingers through his hair. He found a twig and began to scratch designs into the dirt. The last thing Hayes was going to do, Sam realized, was answer his father.

The banjo music shifted to a hard-driving guitar riff, and Ryder said, "Damn bastard. What a little punk. Here I come all the way out here and—"

A rumble stopped him.

Sam heard it and so did Hayes. Both boys placed flat palms against the desert floor and waited. It started far off, like a sound from a film, but soon it was right under them, a thunderous calling from the deep—the ground shook beneath them. An earthquake. Sam watched as his mother turned to the blue awning, which swung back and forth. She backed away as if the trailer were alive. Ryder sat back in his truck and shook his head.

The ground shook for thirty seconds. Sam closed his eyes and counted... One Mississippi. Two Mississippi. Three Mississippi...

When all was still, Ryder lifted a middle finger at the boys— well, in their general direction—and spun the truck back toward his cabin in a cloud of dust and churning gravel. He floored the engine, and the white truck edged along the desert floor, spun into an S-turn, and vanished.

Sam's mom waddled into the trailer—the door slammed behind her.

Hayes continued to sketch with his twig. This was, as far as Sam could remember, how he always ran into Ryder Simms. The man was either yelling, screaming, or cursing at somebody. Often, it was Hayes. But Sam stayed away from the man, always far off, distant. Like a coyote, loose from the pack, watching a predator's hungry, insistent fury. Again, Sam stood without making a sound. The desert-shrub cough once lodged in his throat was gone, and he began to slowly—ever so slowly—back away from the closest friend he had in the whole wide world. *Maybe*, Sam thought, *I really will find some way to scare Hayes today.*

What I think I'll do, if I can hide long enough, is wait until it gets dark.

5

Sam downshifted into second gear and, as the old Chevy slowed, his teeth rattled like the truck's undercarriage. *Something isn't right down there*, Sam thought. *I need to take a look.* Alignment. Suspension. Balance. It all went to hell as the years unfolded. A hundred or so feet ahead—dead center in the two-lane blacktop—a lone coyote paused and swiveled its head toward Sam and his Chevy. It was a skinny creature. Brindle patches of fur jutted from between its shoulder blades. Its front and hind legs appeared, to Sam, more twig than flesh and bone. Small, too. Rat-like and skittish, moving like an underworld specimen, the coyote hunched into the pavement, lowered its head and slid its lips upward to reveal yellow dog teeth caked with spittle.

Sam pressed in the clutch, downshifted into first, and applied the brakes. His Chevy came to a stop, sat shaking in the desert's dry coldness. East and west, along the highway, the desert unspooled beneath a gray sky layered with flat, slow-moving clouds. To the east, spread like pockmarks, lay boxy homes surrounded by chain-link and rusted machinery husks of broken-down automobiles. To the west? A few homes framed by knife-blade mountains. Serrated peaks backlit by off-colored distance. Everything appeared washed in gray. A hell of a winter. *It sure might snow,* Sam thought again. It would surprise him if it didn't. Once or twice a year it came, and when it did, Sam knew, there was always a chance it could fall thick—you never thought so, not with this landscape, but it happened. Sam lifted his right palm toward the heater vent, squeezed his hand into a fist and released it. The heat licked at his mangled palm.

Through the dusty windshield, he watched the coyote move forward and, an instant later, freeze. Sam squinted, caught a flash from each side of the creature's head. "You've got gray eyes," Sam said, "don't you?" His mind touched on the gun hidden beneath his seat, a Luger, one Hayes had left to him before going to war. Sam still remembered the cold, heavy feel of the gun when Hayes handed it to him. He'd said, "It's like a paperweight or something."

And Hayes, his eyes burning with mayhem, had said, "That's no paperweight, Sam. You can use that gun, right there, to kill whatever the hell you think needs killing."

"Whoever," Sam said.

"That's right... Whoever and whatever."

Sam had used the gun once—once, he had thought, would be enough. But he had an urge, looking at the coyote, to lift the gun and point it, to feel that stiff kick from the simple action of squeezing the trigger.

And the animal had done nothing to him. Not a damn thing. The coyote hovered on the pavement, scissored its legs, and drifted into the brush beside the highway—vanished.

Sam released the clutch and feathered the throttle. The Chevy lurched forward amid groans and squeaks from its metal pieces, shuddered until it reached a respectable speed. Sam's eyes shot to the rearview mirror, lingered on the barren highway splitting the horizon.

He thought to himself: *Why'd the coyote cross the road?*

»»»»»

A percussive thump punched at Sam's ears as he turned east down the dirt road toward Hayes's house. He stopped the Chevy and rolled down the window. Cold bit the skin on his face, burned his lips and cheeks. The temperature hovered in the midtwenties. Not bad, but it still made Sam's lungs clench and the muscles in his back tighten. What was that thump? It sifted through the air like smoke, floated across the spiny tops of Joshua trees and cacti, and landed in the Chevy's cab. *A beat,* Sam told himself. *It's music, pal.* He thought so: It was good old rock 'n' roll—no doubt in his mind. He squinted through the trees, tried to make out the cabin that he knew sat on five acres a half mile from the highway.

The two-bedroom place—where his buddy Hayes grew up—was built by hand during the late thirties. Back then, there was no highway. It took four-wheel drive and some real steel-coated balls to get up there. Sam figured whoever built the place brought the cinder blocks and cement mix in on a mule. He couldn't see the flat, tarp-covered roof, but he spotted a thin trail of gray smoke rising like thread into the sky.

So, Sam thought, *Hayes is back and he's listening to a little music. See, it's all good. It's all going to be fine. Hayes is back and he's good as new. Shoot, better.* Sam shook his head and reminded himself that Hayes had his quirks, that being better than new might mean being worse than before—if there was such a thing. Sam did not understand—not completely—his fear of Hayes. He expected silence, and that was fine. Silence was silence. It wasn't death or hatred or anything worse than itself. *It's the secret you keep pushing away, Sam. That's exactly what it is—now, you have something to hide from Hayes.*

And you want to know how you'll do it.

How do you hide the worst thing you've ever done from the best friend you've ever known? Can you hide it? Is it possible? *You keep your mouth shut, that's what you do.* Sam breathed in a large gulp of cold air. He closed his eyes and let the burn fill his lungs and throat. In that moment, with the cold air filling his body, guilt ran through Sam's blood. He felt it in every nerve, every cell, and every thought. Nausea spread through him like heat, and the cold vanished. *My god,* Sam thought, *you have nothing to feel but guilt. That's all there is. Guilt, guilt, and more guilt.* It was Hayes who went to war, Hayes who had a father who beat him to pieces. It was Hayes who grew up in the barest version of a home. And it was Hayes who'd put Erin and Sam together, pointed them to each other.

Hayes got so little for his labors, and Sam took all the profits.

He remembered: Erin, the first and last girl he'd ever kissed.

Well, she'd kissed him because Hayes wouldn't have anything to do with her. The son of a gun looked right past her and she walked right into Sam. Sometimes it was better to be lucky, especially with women.

Erin was so damn pretty. She had blue eyes—just like Hayes— and her skin was almond-colored, like the coat of a quarter horse. Long blonde hair, too. She used to smile at the two of them when they pulled into the high school parking lot. Back then, Hayes was already driving his old Dodge Dart. The floorboards were rusted to hell and the body looked like it was held together with Bondo and duct tape, but it sounded sexy. Sam could admit to that.

That car had sounded sexy. Probably still did.

Those old engines, man. These days it's about fuel economy and highway miles. Better that way, but it sure isn't cool. The way Hayes drove at that time set all the girls off—at least the ones who were impressed by that sort of thing. Small-town girls.

Hayes had kept his elbow pointed out the open window and lowered his fake Ray-Bans along the bridge of his nose. Their goal was to look tough, like they didn't care about a damn thing. It's about the best you can do when you're from a small town— look tough and mean because, well, Sam didn't know why. It's what you did.

How it happened: Erin came up to them one day as Hayes slid the Dodge Dart into a parking space in the high school lot. She tossed her hair across her shoulders, and Sam caught sunlight glinting off it through his sunglasses. Everything looked basted in gold that day. Bright as hell out, a few weeks before summer, their last year in high school. Erin wore her cheerleader uniform and red lipstick Sam knew she hid from her mom.

Hayes leaned his head out the window and removed his sunglasses, hung them from his white V-neck. Sam swore, the guy thought he was God's gift, but that was Hayes in high school, real confident. He shut the car down and turned his lips down at her. "Can we help you, Erin?"

She put both her hands on the door, and Sam noticed her pink fingernails. "You know about prom coming up, Hayes?" She tapped her fingers against the door. She was a little bit nervous, Sam guessed. "It's in a couple weeks, you know. Not too far off to plan—"

"Coming up quick," Hayes said.

"I still don't have anybody to go with."

"Sorry to hear that. I'm sure someone'll come along."

Hayes dropped a bomb on her dream just like that. Real asshole-like.

Sam watched Erin coax a smile from the folds of deep sorrow on her face. "I thought we could go together. That is, if you don't already have a date."

"I ain't going to the dance. I don't like the music."

"It's dance music."

"They should play more country and blues."

"But it's hard to dance to those songs."

Hayes took the sunglasses from his shirt, unfolded and slipped them back over his eyes. "I just don't care about pop music. Like I said, I can't go. You mind, Erin?"

She stumbled backward in the sunlight and her jaw dropped, hung like an ornament. Sam saw she was stunned. A beautiful girl like Erin, she was one of those who could have anything she wanted in this life on looks alone. The type: all-American good looks, but sweet, too. And smart. Sam could tell you about Erin going to college, but that's a story that never happened.

Not in this life, it didn't.

Hayes had opened the door, grabbed his books, and walked toward first-period class, not a care in his world. Times like that, Sam saw Hayes as a real bastard. It wasn't that Hayes didn't care for people, or feel what they felt. No—it was that he couldn't be bothered with the small things, with the little bit of kindness that it took to make others feel alive day after day. Sam climbed out, slammed the door, and walked around the car. "Sorry about him. Maybe he didn't get his beauty sleep."

Erin tilted her head at him and squinted, a tinge of mischief in her eyes. Not desire, but daring and mischief, and maybe recognition or a little light turning on when it shouldn't. Real loud, she said, "Sam, you are one handsome motherfucker."

Sam shrugged and laughed—he didn't know what to say to that.

Erin looked toward Hayes. He stopped for a moment and turned to watch. She fell into Sam, and every cell in his body lifted and sang. His heart lunged in his chest. He looked down at Erin, and her lips came toward his. Sam bent a little and there it was... Her tongue darted out and touched his teeth, probed. He sent his tongue back and a charge screamed from Sam's throat to Erin's, their own bridge of white heat.

It felt good. Damn good. But Sam's first worry was Hayes. *I mean,* Sam thought, *what the hell is this?* When Erin pulled away, Sam turned to look at Hayes. But Erin reached up and grabbed Sam's chin with one hand, swung his head back to hers. For a good clear second, they stared at each other. Sam remembered his own wavering reflection in her blue eyes.

There he was, caught inside her like a whirlpool.

Hayes said, "Get some, Sam. That a boy."

Sam peeled his thoughts from the past's tacky surface, rolled up the window, and let the Chevy coast down the dirt track lined with creosote and small yucca trees. Funny how things worked in this world. Now, Sam was married to Erin. He yanked the wheel to dodge a head-sized boulder. The truck's suspension protested but settled back over the wheels. As he got closer, the beat grew in intensity, boiled over until it throbbed in the air. A high-hat started in and Sam knew the beat, a soul or blues number. *Who is that? I know that song. I just need to hear the voice.* As he rounded the corner, Sam's breath caught in his throat.

A lump grew in him, centered itself below his chin like a tumor.

Flanking the dirt lane on both sides were barriers built from sandbags. The sandbags were stacked about four feet high and spread about ten to twelve feet in width. In each barrier's center, a small opening allowed space for a man to point a weapon at trespassers. This here was new. Used to be a fallen chain-link fence flanking this road. Now it was, what was the word? Now it was *fortified*. That's what Sam imagined Hayes would tell him, *"It's fortified Sam, what do you say to that?"*

Sam cleared his throat. "Oh, Hayes," he said to the cold air. "I don't like the looks of this." He slammed his palm against the Chevy's horn and rolled down his window again, leaned his head into the biting desert air and shouted, "Hayes, you in there? You drunk or just acting stupid?" He laid on the horn for thirty seconds, stopped. The music kept on, transitioned into piano-laden chords, rattled into a verse. The voice that burned through the air was none other than the late, great Elvis Presley. The damn king. Sam grinned and shook his head.

Yeah, Hayes was back alright.

Fortified and electrified, so to speak.

A tap sounded against the back window.

Sam swung his head to the left and came face-to-face with a shotgun. His stomach dropped through his ass. He gulped, pivoted his gaze past the black tunnel where—if fired—the shell would plunge at its target, and pasted his eyes on the face that hovered above the gun.

Hayes.

His black hair ran stringy and caked down the sides of his head. His eyes were bloodshot, unstable in their sockets. His same strong, angled nose pointed off to the left, a minor readjustment. On his forehead, above his left eye, an irregular-shaped bruise shown deep black. A half grin spread from the center of his mouth, and he said, "You sure do make lots of noise."

"Bad habit, I guess."

Hayes lifted the shotgun—a pump-action Remington, Sam noticed—and rested it across one shoulder. He squinted at Sam and rolled his head from side to side. He cocked an ear and listened to the music, Elvis Presley booming out lyrics against the insistent plunk of bass guitar and zealous piano. "This man,

I'll tell you what. He could sing the clothes off a mannequin. No doubt in my mind."

Sam nodded. He tried to arrange his thoughts against the music's thunderous onslaught, told himself, *I can't think my way through a bad joke, all this noise.* Maybe he should ask Hayes to turn it down or, hell, turn it off for the time being. Instead, Sam said, "What album is this?"

Hayes teetered on his feet, moved the shotgun to his other shoulder. *"From Elvis in Memphis.* Nothing but blues and soul and love. It's the comeback album, is what it is. None of that shit-for-nothing crap he did the few years before. You know, all those movies he did, pretty face all done up like a prince. This is good music, this album. Got soul."

"No shit? I think I heard this a few years back. You played it for me."

"You can bet your ass. I played you all the good stuff. Nothing but." Hayes closed one eye and studied him. He grunted and slapped a hand on the Chevy's door. "I'm glad to see you, Sam. It's been a while, right? Well, here we are." Hayes pulled his eyes from Sam, shot a glance toward the sandbags, and said, "Welcome home."

Sam clenched his teeth and thought: *Hell, I'm the one's supposed to say that.* The music filled the air with hard chords and long vowels.

Hayes ran his tongue across his chapped lower lip, turned and ambled toward the opening between the sandbags. All at once, the music ended, crushed itself into silence with one brief, thunderous crescendo. Hayes lowered the shotgun, held it across his chest, and called in a clear voice, "Come on in, Sam. Don't be shy around your old friend."

Comes a time, you know you won't make it. You know—no matter what the fuck happens out here—it's not the same You going back home. You, you know? There's no more You. It's like when a rattlesnake sheds its skin. The dead skin, without the flesh and the bone and the venom, lies there in the dirt. Empty. It's useless.

Toss. Plunge.

FNG over there won't stop with the foxhole. He won't stop with the shovel. With the dirt. With the grave he's digging for himself.

I say, fuck it all to hell. Go ahead, FNG. Dig that foxhole.

One grave is as good as the next.

Toss. Plunge. Toss. Plunge.

He's waist-deep now, putting his back into it. I can hear him grunting with the effort, smell his sweat as it mixes with the godforsaken dust of this earth. See, FNG over there still thinks he's going to make it. Still thinks he'll be himself when he gets back to Bumfuck, Nevada, Ohio, Georgia. Or wherever the hell his people call home. He thinks little miss homecoming queen is still going to want a nice long suck on his pecker. He thinks he's got a job waiting for him. He thinks he's got a big bank account and a nice shiny pickup truck in his future.

Toss. Plunge.

FNG still hopes his life is his own.

But it's not. No, sir. His life—and mine—belongs to good, old Uncle Sam. And Uncle Sam has needs, motherfuckers. He's got addictions.

Toss. Plunge.

Uncle Sam's got the hunger.

"You hear that, FNG?" I ask him a question every once in a while, and the man won't answer. Nope. No talky mumbo jumbo

for FNG.

He digs and he sweats. All there is to the man: dirt and sweat.

And a hole getting deeper by the hour.

"I ever tell you about how I joined the Corps, FNG?" I say it loud enough so he can hear over his shovel biting into the dirt. "It's a story, FNG." It's a goddamn tooth-knocking, chin-splitting, heart-bursting hell of a story.

FNG doesn't answer.

He's digging. All he does is dig.

"Fuck you, FNG," I say. "Fuck you for digging. Why don't you put that shovel down and listen to my story? Come sit around the campfire.

"Alright, no can do, huh? All you want to do is sweat. Say, FNG, what is it you want on your tombstone? You can tell me.

"Nope? Okay, forget it. I'll go first: Here Lies..."

Shit, I had it just the other day—I had a dream about my damn tombstone.

Toss. Plunge.

What the fuck was it? Something about glory. Or honor. Or another fancy horseshit word they say in the newspaper all the time. You know the kind of word I'm talking about? It's a spelling-test word. The fuck was that word?

"I got one for you, FNG. How about: Here Lies FNG. Died before his time.

"You can keep that one, FNG. I'll let you have it."

He won't listen. This son-of-a-bitch FNG will not listen to me.

Toss. Plunge. Toss. Plunge.

It's the same sounds over and over again:

FNG's shovel biting into dirt. Now and again the volley of machine-gun fire. Distant explosions. Dogs barking.

That shovel.

That goddamn shovel.

PART II
Lone Wolves

6

Sam's eyes did not move from the shotgun as he followed Hayes through the yard. Tilted against his shoulder, the gun jutted at the sky like a splinted finger. It was the third time in Sam's life he'd had a gun pointed at him. Twice, and no more, it was Ryder Simms. Today, Hayes.

First, Sam thought, *lies the father. And second lies the son.* Sam pressed his teeth together, tasted the last bitterness of coffee fading on his tongue.

Hayes labored ahead, grunted with effort as he moved through the desert toward the cinder-block structure. Sam said, "You on watch, or what?"

"Just out for a stroll," Hayes said without turning. "I got bad knees now. They made me an old man in the Marine Corps. I bet you didn't see that coming." He stopped, straightened his neck, and turned his head to the south. The shotgun swiveled down and pointed at a gray, half-rusted vehicle—the Dodge Dart. A few warped two-by-fours lay against the hood, and the passenger-side front tire was flat—the car sat angled in the dirt, like a confidence man's crooked smile. "I got that sucker running, by the way. I just need to change the front tire and we can go for a ride."

Sam, the collar of his coat lifting in the slight breeze, cleared his throat and said, "I still think it needs a paint job, Hayes."

"Who cares how it looks?" Hayes shrugged. The shotgun wavered, swung back to his shoulder and its big target in the sky. "All that matters is the sucker starts up and runs."

Like Hayes, Sam loved the Dodge Dart. Looking at it, a nostalgia overtook him. He lamented the days before Reagan came, and the days before Hayes joined the Marine Corps. Sam saw life as spit-shined with promise, bursting at the seams with teenage certainty—he was going to be somebody, or something.

Somehow. Some damn day. And, sure, he didn't know what he was going to be. Or what he could be. But Sam craved that feeling of possibility, the precious notion that the future still lay ahead of him, a promise to himself that he was not simply a small-town kid afflicted with cowardice. Maybe what Sam wanted—for all those years as a child and young adult—was to be a hero, like Hayes. How fast the years had unraveled and left him sprawling at memory, glaring up at life as if from the floor of a bare-knuckle boxing ring. What remained of the days before the war and the birth of Sam's son, was the Dodge Dart—all else had changed. There was the sound the car made, a dedicated and faulty rumble that Sam equated with thunder. There was the way it shivered when you yanked a too-hard left turn, the way it spat exhaust on acceleration, left a white cloud hovering at every four-way stop.

He remembered that it was a cold spring morning when Hayes had slapped six hundred dollars in fives and twenties into Old Man Saber's callused right hand. The old man had counted the wrinkled bills with deliberate gestures, his lips mouthing the numbers, and smiled at Hayes and Sam when he finished. He looked back at the primer-gray Dodge Dart behind him—it sat in ankle-length grass beside a barn-red mobile home—and said, "It still runs like a champ. I even changed the oil a few weeks back."

Sam, for his part, thought the old man was lying—the Dodge's windshield was cracked on the lower half and covered with a winter's worth of grime and dust. He had his doubts about the car, but Hayes had few options. He'd made eight hundred bucks doing construction over the winter break, and he wanted a car. Well, to be more precise, Hayes said he wanted a "muscle car."

The Dodge was muscle alright, Sam thought, weary muscle.

Before handing over his hard-earned cash, Hayes had grinned at the old man and hopped into the driver's seat. When he started the engine, a cloud of blue smoke shot from the muffler. He gave it some throttle and the engine made a sound like a giant power drill backing out rusted screws. He poked his head out the window. "You hear that, Sam? Pretty, huh?"

The old man looked at Sam. His face was slack and expectant. "It runs," Sam said.

"You're damn right it runs." The old man shuffled toward the Dodge and prodded the hood with a finger. "I had this since 1971, August 1971. Treated it like my own child. You won't find a seal or a valve on this sucker has any kind of leak. This sucker is like new. You can take it from me."

Sam went to one knee and peered beneath the car. Spider webs stretched from the tires to the shock absorbers, from the undercarriage to the rusty muffler's snake-like meanderings. "It doesn't look like you drive it much."

"What do I need to go to town for? Why would I go down there?"

Sam stood and lifted the hood. Hayes left the Dodge running and joined Sam and the old man as they gazed into the car's hot-breathing innards.

"You can't hear a lifter at all," the old man said. "You know what kind of maintenance that takes? A fine hand and eye, that's what kind—dedication, boys." He grunted and lifted a finger to the tip of his nose, scratched.

Hayes said, "Man, I love this thing. It's exactly what I want."

"We should take it to Ralph, over in town, let him have a look at it."

"Oh, come on, Sam. What's Ralph going to say? It needs work? Shit, you and me both know that."

The old man said, "It doesn't need nothing but a driver."

Sam walked around to the car's rear and watched puffs of white smoke leave the muffler. "You think this means anything, Hayes?"

"It's cold out. That's all it means." The old man was more than irritated. "You're not buying this sucker, anyhow. Let your pal here ask the questions."

Sam shrugged and thought: *It's his money. Not mine.*

Later, there had been a wildness in Hayes as the Dodge roared down the two-lane highway. He had the window rolled down and his left elbow dangled into the ice-cold air. Sam shivered and scratched at points of numb flesh on his cheeks. "You mind shutting that window? My face is frozen."

Hayes rolled his eyes and pumped the hand crank.

With the windows closed, the Dodge sounded like a monsoon. Sam marked the car's flaws. The dashboard was cracked in three places, rust had burned through the floorboard, the vinyl bench seat was spilling foam stuffing, and the door to the glove compartment wouldn't stay closed. This was all superficial, Sam knew, but it signaled something about the rest of the vehicle. "Man," he said, "I worry you just wasted your money."

"Sam, you need to grow a pair. Can't you feel the power in this sucker?" Hayes shook his head and swung the wheel as they crested a rise and loped into a hairpin turn. Beneath them, the Dodge's suspension groaned. "I know you're afraid"—he laughed—"and that you don't know how to man up, but look at us, will you? We're in a damn muscle car and we're going to ride around town and have everybody look at us."

"And they'll laugh themselves to death." Sam didn't care much about that. For him, it was a matter of taking unnecessary risks. The Dodge wasn't proven. "You didn't think the old man was lying?"

Hayes shrugged. He poked the radio and power guitar chords burned through static. He bobbed his head and mimicked the last phrase in the chorus: "And-fire-in-the-sky-I. You know," he said, "my dad bought that International pickup from him when I was a kid. It still runs perfect, and all he has to do is get new tires once a year. Well, used-new tires. I think he might have changed the spark plugs."

Sam sensed the speedometer inching higher as they came out of the sharp turn. He winced at the repetitive bar chords droning from the Dodge's speakers. *Such a simple song.* Up ahead, there was a two-mile stretch in the road. More or less straight, but dimpled with occasional dips. The road was maintained by the county and, even after a rough winter, it was smooth and flat as bathroom tile. Hayes gave it more gas and the car's monsoon sound heightened against guitar and drums and bass. Sam said, "You mind slowing down a little bit? Who knows what's wrong with this thing, Hayes."

Hayes ignored him. The engine roared and wind hissed through the windows where—over many years—heat had worn away their seals. Sam flashed on the time they stole the Ford truck. Like then, on the rough dirt road, his fingers slipped beneath the Dodge's bench seat and bit into the steel. He didn't want to pray, but some part of him craved it. Ahead, the road dipped and leveled at imprecise distances. "Hayes, you need to slow down."

"No, sir," Hayes said. He brought his other hand to the wheel and squinted into the sunlight, pushed the Dodge harder, as if he were a jockey headed toward a photo finish—the Dodge sank into the road's first depression.

For an instant, the car seemed weightless, but it sank heavily into the tired suspension. Creaks sprang from beneath their feet. As the Dodge's hood pointed skyward, Hayes started to grin. They came out of the depression and, where the sun hit the road like a spotlight, a brindle blur flitted at the edges of Sam's vision. "Hayes—stop!"

Hayes punched the brakes and the Dodge's tires—sun-faded and weak in the sidewalls—squealed in Sam's ears. The Dodge slid forward like a bullet. After what felt like forever, the vehicle spun counterclockwise. A gunshot sounded beneath them and the Dodge tilted. Next, sounds like laundry flapping on a clothesline penetrated the engine's decaying monsoon—the Dodge creaked, groaned, and rolled to a stop. Sam stared through the dusty windshield at a lone coyote. The animal lowered its head, studied them with beady-eyed concentration, and darted into the desert beyond sight.

"That son of a gun almost got us killed," Hayes said. His hands were white-knuckled around the steering wheel, and the muscles in his cheeks were clenched like biceps. He turned to Sam—there was a brightness in his eyes, a sheen like cold water on a knife blade.

Sam said, "*You* almost got us killed."

"I think you mean to say it the other way around: I saved us."

"Now we know the brakes are working."

Hayes grunted an affirmation. "Well, we got our first flat tire out of the way. You want to change it, or should I?"

Sam didn't answer. Instead, he thought along with the radio, and fire... in the sky-I.

That day, after changing a flat tire on a stretch of cold vacant highway, was the day Sam had first spoken to Ryder Simms. All the years he'd spent with Hayes, and Sam had never spoken to his buddy's father. Seemed like Ryder always skipped town when it came time for back-to-school days or parent-teacher conferences, or when all the kids their age met at the pizza parlor for birthday parties. Hayes caught rides into town with friends who lived nearby and, when he got older, he hitchhiked. To Sam, Ryder was a ghost, but on that day he proved himself flesh and blood.

The Dodge bumped down the dirt lane with dust lifting behind it. Hayes slid to a stop near the white pickup truck that sat alongside the cinder-block cabin. By the time he shut off the engine and he and Sam were squinting beneath the hood, Ryder was outside, a pistol lashed to his thigh and a green trucker's hat shading his deep-set eyes. His white tank top was yellowed around his ribs, and he didn't bother with a belt to cinch his Levi's, or a coat against the brisk wind. Ryder looked like a hobo, the way his hair spilled in white tufts over his ears, sprang unhindered from beneath the mesh hat and fell down his thin and pasty neck.

Sam watched as he ambled toward the Dodge.

Ryder's hand went to the pistol, rested there. "Who's this pansy?"

Without looking at his father, Hayes said, "This is my buddy, Sam. You know who he is. He lives down the road... We've known each other forever."

Sam nodded slightly, cast his eyes beyond Ryder and his handy pistol.

Ryder approached, held out a hand and Sam took it. "Ain't had the formal pleasure, I guess. You boys got yourself a muscle car, huh?"

Hayes said, "It runs good, too. We got it from Old Man Saber."

"That's where I got my truck, but you got to watch him—he'll try and cheat you. Just like everybody else."

As Ryder brushed by him, Sam smelled gunpowder and bacon grease. He didn't know why, but the hair on his neck prickled. "I tried to warn Hayes, but he wanted the damn thing too much."

Ryder said, "How much you pay for this piece of junk?"

"Three hundred bucks," Hayes lied.

Sam's eyes shot to Hayes. He didn't understand the need for the lie.

Ryder groaned and crossed his arms over his chest. "I know that old bastard wouldn't let you take this off him for less than five hundred." He rotated his gaze from the engine to the back of his son's tan neck. "Did you just lie to me? I sure hope you didn't lie to me, boy."

Sam sensed danger in that moment. He watched Ryder's fingers grip the sides of his arms and he noticed Hayes tense his shoulders, like a fullback about to plunge toward a stacked goal line.

Hayes rubbed the back of his head. "I said three hundred, and that's what it was. You're always trying to make me a liar."

Ryder unfolded his arms, lifted a hand, and slapped Hayes on the back of the neck—the skin there blushed red. Hayes tilted forward with the blow, caught himself on the Dodge's metal grill and straightened. As he turned, Ryder slapped Hayes in the face. Ryder's flat hand against his son's cheek sounded like a flag unwrapping in a stiff wind. "What'd I tell you about lying to me?"

"Don't do it."

"Right," Ryder said. He gripped Hayes by the collar of his coat. "How much was this piece of junk?"

Sam thought of his own father. He saw the man sleeping in the travel trailer where they lived, a threadbare blanket draped across his knees and a half-empty bottle of cheap wine beside him. Sam's father was a ghost to him. To be hit, for Sam, would have been proof of love, or hate, or anything that meant emotion. "It was six hundred even." Sam heard his own voice, but he didn't know where it came from—he spoke without trying.

Ryder let Hayes go and stepped backward into the sunlight. His crumpled lips unfolded, and he screeched a high-pitched laugh. "Six hundred for this piece of shit? Oh, boy, you got taken for a ride. He should have paid you to take this old thing." He leaned under the hood and studied the contours of the hissing engine. "Let me guess, you got white smoke from the exhaust, am I right?"

Hayes stared at Sam over Ryder's bent frame. With one hand, he rubbed the back of his neck. He looked only at Sam when he spoke: "A little bit of white smoke. It's nothing I can't fix on my own."

"You know I'm not going to be much help. I'm too old for this shit. I bet you the six hundred, you got a bad head gasket. It might not go for a while, but you can bet it will someday. Soon, too." He tossed his head, adjusted the green trucker's hat, and walked without ceremony toward the porch. He climbed the steps one at a time, a queer patience animating his motions. Before vanishing inside the dark doorway, he said, "You got a lemon, boy. Let that be a lesson to you—never buy a car without a man present. Otherwise, you end up with a big, sour nothing."

Sam did not look at his friend. Instead, he stared for a long time at the pockmarked desert stretching yawn-like to the horizon.

Six years later, outside that same cabin, Sam stared into that same dark doorway. Set at opposite ends of the wide cement porch, Hayes had two speakers wired up—power ran into them from wires stretching through the gaping blackness. Hayes stomped his feet as he ascended the four steps to the front door, lifted his shoulders slightly, and vanished into the darkness. He cut the music from inside, and the desert's cold silence seemed louder than the speakers. He shouted, "Come on in!"

Sam climbed the steps and hesitated at the door. Another memory prodded at his mind's edge: that gravel-laden voice and white hair above a hawk-featured face. Ryder with a pistol in his hand and a leering grin shining through dim light. Staring through the doorway, into the blackness beyond, Sam felt his scarred jaw develop a phantom ache. Another memory, later: Ryder toppled over, a rifle lazy and useless in his arms, blood seeping through his flannel shirt. Sam shook away these thoughts, forced them deeper into his mind.

From inside, Hayes said, "My daddy's gone, Sam. Come on in. He can't hurt you." A short, halfhearted laugh surfaced and died against the cabin's cinder-brick walls.

Sam stepped through the doorway. In one corner, Hayes had the wood stove burning hot. The heat flashed against Sam's face, drew him toward its source. What Sam remembered of the place—a pack rat's dream of magazines and newspapers and odds and ends—was replaced with the current furnishings. Or lack thereof. Against the far wall was a camping cot with a green sleeping bag rolled tight at one end. A blue container for drinking water sat beneath the cot and, to one side, a small camp stove rested atop a footlocker. Stamped across the footlocker, barely visible in what little light filtered through the doorway: USMC. The rest of the place was bare, little more than a cinder-block prison cell. The small kitchen range and sink that once stood along the wall opposite the wood stove were both gone. Small holes remained for the gas line and plumbing. Sam watched as Hayes bent to one knee, twisted a latch, and shoved a piece of firewood into the wood burner. He slammed the door, latched it tight, and stood to face Sam. The shotgun was cradled like a child in his arms. "It warms up quick in here, doesn't it?"

Sam said, "I love what you've done with the place."

"I never did worry about being comfortable."

Sam nodded. He drifted toward the front window and its thick blanket covering. With his index finger, Sam pried at the covering—some kind of wool fabric—and tried to make a crack through which he could see the desert.

"You mind?" Hayes said. "Don't mess with that. I like it dark in here."

"Why's that?"

"I just do. You got a problem with it?"

"No, sir."

"Don't you call me sir."

Sam lowered his hand, shoved it into the front pocket of his Levi's. With his other hand, he scratched the back of his head. But the music—*where the hell had that come from?* He scoured the threadbare carpet beneath his feet. Followed a black cord to where it reached a spot behind the footlocker. "A laptop?"

Hayes looked puzzled. "What?"

Sam nodded toward the doorway. "Elvis," he said.

"Oh, yeah. I have a small one right here," Hayes said, and looked toward the cot. "I keep things simple now. That's how I like it."

"That's a way to describe it. Hayes, what in the hell is with—"

"I don't need your damn advice. Not up for taking shit from you, neither."

"Fine." Sam moved toward the door in what he hoped was an

absent-minded manner. The shotgun looked more ominous in the dark somehow, more foreboding and dangerous. "What do we talk about then?"

"You want to sit?" Hayes pointed the shotgun at the cot. "Go ahead."

"Nope. I'm fine right here. It's no problem." A cold wind blew through the doorway, traveled up Sam's spine and made him drift closer to the hot stove.

"Whatever you say. Hey, how's the little one doing?"

An image of Reagan drifted into Sam's head: Reagan stumbled across the apartment, a loose chorus of high-pitched laughs coming from him when he fell onto the carpet. Sam imagined holding his son, how it felt to clutch the small body to his chest, press the two beings—father and son—into each other like flour into stone. He had a recurring thought: *And second lies the son.* A thing he couldn't name told Sam to change the subject, to escape this line of questioning. "Good. Reagan's doing good. What the hell have you been eating out here, jackrabbits and lizards?"

"And canned beans. I shot a coyote a few days ago. Son of a gun kept coming around and I had to make him pay. No good to eat, though."

Sam shook his head. He flashed on the coyote he'd just seen crossing the highway.

Hayes interrupted Sam's thoughts and said, "One thing I wanted to ask you... Is he still around, the recruiter?"

"You're talking about Jazz?"

"That's right. You remember him?"

I saw him this morning, Sam wanted to say, but he caught himself. "Jazz is still around. A while back we used to hang together, go out for a drink now and again. He used to always come into the diner, but that was before—"

"You had the accident." Hayes tensed, lifted the shotgun to his shoulder. His fingers drummed the stock, and his tongue darted across his lips. "You seen him lately?"

Sam lied: "Not for a little while. Why?"

Another puzzled look crossed Hayes's face. He seemed perplexed by the question, like a child surprised by a new math equation. He cleared his throat and gently shifted the shotgun from one shoulder to the other. In a clear, distinct voice, Hayes said, "I'm going to kill the motherfucker—that's why." His gray-pink tongue ran across his bottom lip and retracted. "You sure you don't want to have a seat, Sam? You're making me nervous over there."

Hayes shuffled toward the cot, bent down, and poked at the laptop with a finger. A plodding kick drum came though the speakers, filled in by some keys and decorated by skilled guitar. And then came a voice: the muscular Jim Morrison on high-octane. The song took Sam to another time, years before when that old Dodge Dart roared like a monsoon, and Jim Morrison's same voice groaned at them through the speakers, insisted that love hides.

Teenaged Hayes, behind the wheel, had said, "It's an old pistol, but it's my pistol—I'll be damned if I'm gonna let the old man keep it from me." He punched the throttle and the Dodge's engine protested beneath the hood, sputtered once, and shot forward with a large gulp of gasoline. They rounded a corner and turned north, headed toward the cabin and Ryder Simms.

Sam scratched his teenage, peach-fuzz mustache and tugged at his shirt collar. It was already hot—three-quarters through spring and the desert felt like a different planet. He punched a button to lower the stereo's volume and said, "I swear it's hot. Can you imagine what it'll be this summer?"

"You bitch too much." Hayes shook his head and checked the mirrors. Nothing but desert in the rearview. "Move to Alaska, you can bitch about the weather."

"The last thing I'd do is move to Alaska."

"You know how tough it is to live up there?"

"It's not easy."

Hayes adjusted his position in the driver's seat, draped his left elbow out the window. As the car gained speed, he raised his voice against the wind. "That's how a man lives: You got to catch enough meat before winter, get enough firewood. It's real living, you know? None of this going to the store bullshit or target shooting. You use a bullet, it better hit some kind of animal, some kind of game."

"Listen to you."

"I'm not lying to you. There's no stores in Alaska, not out in the bush, wherever. It's just you and the bears—how a man lives."

"I'm saying it's hot in the desert. It doesn't have a damn thing to do with Alaska." Sam cleared his throat and looked at Hayes, caught the flash of sunlight from his friend's dark sunglasses, the slight smirk on one side of his mouth. "What do you want with the pistol, anyhow? What do you need it for?"

"Target practice, man. What do you think?" They reached a steep grade, and the Dodge lurched and slowed. Hayes groaned before pressing the gas pedal to the floor. "Come on, sister. Take us to the top." The car shifted its low growl to a high-pitched roar—made Sam think of a helicopter—and gripped the pavement, shot them skyward. "Plus, it's my gun and it should be in my possession. Possession is nine-tenths of the law, my man."

"I guess I wonder why you need practice, that's all."

"Jesus... I need to get good at something, don't I?"

"Yeah," Sam said. "I guess you do."

Hayes never talked about Ryder unless it was to say something about how the man was a drunk, or how he was no good. Sam figured that fact told most of what needed telling. Ryder left Hayes alone for large chunks of time. It wasn't clear what he did or where he went, only that he was gone and—at some point—he was back. Hayes hinted that Ryder had been in the service, that something had happened to him, but Sam didn't push it—you didn't push Hayes when it came to his dad. There was a mystery to Ryder, a horror Sam wanted to understand, but he couldn't see how, not without upsetting his buddy. So, as the Dodge Dart rattled down the dirt road toward the cabin with its blue-tarp roof, Sam felt his nerves awaken. He took a deep breath while

Hayes coughed into a fist.

"You want me to do anything, Hayes?"

"Stay in the car and keep the engine running."

They rounded a bend in the dirt road. Hayes slammed on the brakes when he reached sight of the cabin. He shifted the car into park and whipped off his seat belt. "You keep it running, and I'll be right back. Good?"

"Good."

Hayes slammed his door and marched toward the cabin. When he was halfway to the front door, a hand probed at the front window. The hand pressed flat and a face appeared above it. The man was a blur, but Sam made out his gray-white beard and large black orbs for eyes. The face receded, disappeared. Hayes hesitated, moved forward with his hands shoved deep into his Levi's. The cabin door swung open, slammed against the cinderblock wall, and a long barrel probed at the daylight.

Hayes halted.

Sam unbuckled his seat belt and reached to flip the ignition key into the off position. The Dodge's engine sputtered, fell into silence.

"Yes, sir," came Ryder's voice, "don't think I won't shoot my own son."

Hayes rubbed the back of his neck, settled himself and, loud enough for Sam to hear, said: "I came to get my pistol, Daddy—that's all I want."

"Which one is that?"

"The old one."

A cackle came from inside the cabin. Ryder lowered the rifle but remained in the doorway's deep shadow. "You talking about the Luger I keep under my pillow?"

"You said I could have it, that Grandpa left it for me when he died." Hayes took two slow steps toward the cabin. The rifle lifted, centered on him. He stopped.

"You ever heard a thing called a tall tale, son?"

"What's that got to do with the pistol?"

"I lied to you, that's what. A tall tale's just a lie. It's got extra-special detail, things that make it seem real. Funny thing is, lots of people believe it. Dummies, I suppose."

Sam opened the passenger door and stepped into the heavy spring heat. Sam said, "I think we should go, Hayes."

Ryder's voice grew louder: "Who in the hell is that pansy?"

"That's my buddy Sam. From down the way. You met him before."

"What's his daddy do?" The rifle lifted and fell, seemed to mimic Ryder's words.

Hayes grunted and said, "Nobody knows now. His daddy left a couple years back. Used to work over at Stater Brothers. The grocery."

Ryder laughed. It was an absurd sound, half melodic and half tinged with smoke. "Now that, son, is a kind of story we call a tragedy. It's a boring kind of story, but it's one kind is all. They got all types, you know."

"I know it," Hayes said.

Sam shifted his boots in the dirt, looked past the cabin at the jagged hills guarding the horizon—*those are teeth,* Sam thought. Bulbous clouds drifted into view, appeared to lift with the hot air and sunlight. "I don't give two shits about the man," Sam said. His voice sounded, to his own ears, small and girlish. He wondered if Ryder had heard him. Why did his voice sound like that?

"Oh, yes you do," Ryder said. "You can bet your ass you give a damn or two."

Sam's stomach twisted. The nerves he felt surfaced, pushed through his skin and sent an odd taste into his mouth. "He was no good, my father," Sam said. "That's why I don't give two shits."

That cackle echoed from inside the cabin, leaked like fumes into the desert air. "A boy needs his father," Ryder said. "That's why I stuck around."

Sam's eyes shot to Hayes, who let his shoulders droop and, after a moment, straighten. He cleared his throat. "You're no good, too, Daddy. You know it like I do—isn't that right?"

There was a long silence.

Ryder appeared in the doorway. His bare shoulders and torso filled the door frame. In one hand he held a rifle aimed with nonchalant poise at the Dodge Dart. "You want the pistol, smart-ass? I'll give it to you, but let's have your pansy pal come and get it. You stay right where you are." Ryder lifted the rifle at Hayes, probed the air with it. "You just stay where you are and keep your smart-ass mouth shut."

Hayes turned and met Sam's eyes.

Sam thought: *Oh, hell—if you want the damn pistol, I'll go get the damn pistol.*

"Well," Ryder said in a sing-song taunt, "my casa is your casa—come on up, pansy." He receded into the cabin's shadows.

Sam moved forward, felt himself propelled by feet he couldn't control. The cabin loomed ahead like a mirage. There was a thing inside Sam that tugged downward, tried to anchor him to the dirt, but the gliding continued. He passed Hayes, passed the rusted white pickup truck on balding tires—its body caressed by desert brush and cacti—and placed one booted foot on the cement steps that led to the cabin's front door. *Here goes*, Sam thought. He forced himself toward the door, stopped when the darkness lay there ahead of him like a tunnel. A smell came to him. Burned toast. He sensed gunpowder, too. And potpourri weighted down with the stale tinge of cigarette smoke.

"Come on in, pansy."

Sam moved forward, stepped into the darkness.

The lone front window was covered by a thick purple blanket hanging on bent nails. There was a skeletal futon against a far wall—it lacked a mattress, and Sam could see the steel bars poking into the room's semi-darkness. The floor was matted green carpet strewn with old photographs, newspapers, and thrift-store books. There were short candles in each corner and record covers plastered along the walls. In one corner, a small refrigerator hummed, and its top was covered with dirty plates, cups, forks, and spoons. A set of steak knives waited on a bookshelf next to the humming machine. The shelf was filled with dry goods: pancake mix, maple syrup, half-empty bags of rice, dry beans, and flour. From the back room, Ryder drifted in like a ghost. The rifle hovered at his waist, swiveled in one hand like a sword. "So, your friend out there wants his pistol, huh?"

"I guess he does." Sam spit the words. His mouth was stiff, half locked in one position. "You give it to me, and we're gone. He won't come back until you say it's okay."

"He don't come back until I say, anyhow." Ryder drifted closer to Sam. The man moved like mist, a half-empty silhouette, through the air.

The smell of cigarette smoke amplified. *It's him. That smell is the man himself.* Sam sniffed hard and thought of Hayes as a small boy. They were what, twelve? He remembered Hayes coming to school with a misshapen and swollen left arm, how a teacher took him from class and the next day Hayes showed up with a big white cast. Sam remembered Hayes trading homemade deer jerky for fruit snacks, how he deflated a math teacher's tires and ended up missing the last month of eighth grade. And, worse than all that, Sam remembered Hayes huddling outside their high school during freshman year while he waited for Ryder to pick him up—deep winter and nightfall when Sam got a phone call from Hayes: Did Sam think his mom could give Hayes a ride? It was a long drive, sure, but damn it was cold out there.

So many visions, horror stories. From somewhere deep inside himself, Sam sensed swelling courage. He spoke without realizing what he'd say. And, when it came out, his stomach dropped. He said, "You ever take a shower?"

The refrigerator rattled, sighed, and its humming disappeared. The room was silent and dark. Ryder's mouth moved in the center of his unkempt beard. "Not if I can help it, but that's the pleasure of working from home—ain't it?" Ryder took another step toward Sam, let the rifle swing down alongside his left leg. "I'll tell you what, pansy. I got no trouble with you, but the boy out there... That boy needs another lesson or two, don't you think?"

"No, sir."

"Oh, sure he does."

Ryder moved forward and his breath pressed into the air around Sam's face. The man was a bit taller than Sam, more round in the belly, but his shoulders and arms were pale and thin, like drawings in a children's book. Ryder's right hand went to the small of his back and reappeared with the Luger. It was smaller than Sam imagined, made him think of a child's water gun. "That's it? That's what Hayes wants?" Sam pressed his lips into a line.

Ryder said, "It'll stop your heart if it hits you in the right spot."

"Doesn't look like it."

Ryder shrugged. He lifted the gun above his shoulder.

Sam said, "Why are you holding it like that?"

Ryder grinned. He tensed his shoulder and forearm.

The Luger swiped forward, moved down at lightning speed.

»»»»»

Before Sam opened his eyes, a throb burned through his chin and up the side of his head. With one hand, he touched sticky liquid on the left side of his chin. He forced his eyes to open— sunlight pried at his pupils and he squinted. He was in a place he knew. The Dodge Dart's passenger seat. "What happened?"

A voice floated toward him, echoed somewhere distant. "You got pistol-whipped, buddy. Consider your cherry popped."

Sam's eyes adjusted to the light and, little by little, he made out Hayes in the driver's seat, one arm dangling out the open window. Sam tried to straighten in the seat, but a surging nausea filled his stomach and stretched into his throat. He stopped moving. "Where are we?"

"Just in the desert. Off the highway. I got sick of driving, didn't know where to go." Hayes sniffed hard and cleared his throat. "He's a violent son of a gun, my dad."

To Sam, there was a vague wonder in Hayes's voice. Sam said,

"The fucker hit me as hard as he could."

"Yeah. That's for sure."

"I lose any teeth?"

"Do any teeth feel loose?"

Sam felt along the ridge of his jaw with a hand. None felt loose, but his whole face stung when he touched it. "I don't think so."

"You'll still be ugly. Too damn bad."

"Why'd he do that?"

"My dad? He did it because he's a hate-filled prick. There's no other reason."

Sam took a deep breath, tried to force the nausea away, straightened in his seat. From what he could tell, they were a few miles north of the highway, parked alongside a dirt road. The sun angled west, plummeted toward the horizon. The sky shown clear and purple-tinged at its edges. He saw in his mind the purple-rimmed lids beneath Ryder's hollow eyes. The nausea rose inside Sam again, touched the rawness of his throat. A linked chain of odd thoughts came to him: *I'd like to kill that man. I'd like to bury him in a hole, or leave him out where the buzzards can get to him. He's no good, and why can't I be the one to put him out of his own and everyone else's misery? I could do it if I wanted to, but I'd need to decide how. How? How to kill an old man?* Sam pondered this while he bared his teeth at the pain in his jaw. "How'd you get me out of there?"

Hayes sniffed, ran a finger along the steering wheel as if tracing an image he'd forgotten. "Dragged you out, my man. Did what I needed to do."

"Thanks, Hayes."

"I'm the one got you into that in the first place."

"And you got me out." Sam looked at his left hand. His fingers were red with blood. "Is it still bleeding?"

Hayes looked at him, shrugged. "Not enough to worry about."

"Did we get the pistol?"

Hayes leaned forward, twisted his hand beneath the driver's

seat. He slumped back into the seat and produced the Luger. He held it to the light and bent his head to one side. The gun seemed older in the light, a relic. "You're damn right we got it. You think I'd let that fucker take your dignity and my pistol? Nope, we needed to get something out of that transaction."

Sam shook his head and grinned. His mouth felt stiff, almost frozen. *The gun*, he thought. *I could kill the old man with the gun.* He pushed the thought away and said: "You better hold on to that fucker, or I'm going to shoot you with it, you son of a gun."

8

Killing, Sam once thought, might make him a man. But he'd discovered different—he'd seen how killing made a man into an empty vessel, a fragile shell, void of emotion, purpose, honor. No, killing did not make one a man, and it didn't make one a better husband, father, or friend. Instead, Sam felt that killing—it didn't have to be another man—stripped one of some essential element, a necessary ingredient to the recipe that made a purposeful, full-feeling human. Otherwise, all life was a trek through the past—this is what it was for Sam, a constant refusal at time's ceaseless churning. He knew what it was to live with regret, and to regret to live. How could he tell Hayes the truth? Sit here, in this dark, cinder-brick cell, and tell the man outright? Tell him what he'd done.

No, Sam thought, *I can't—I'm too much of a coward.*

In the dark cabin, now silent, Hayes lowered the Remington into a loose, one-handed grip. He walked slowly past Sam and stepped onto the cabin's porch. Sam turned and studied Hayes in relief against heatless sunlight. The former Marine's shoulder blades jutted wing-like against his flannel shirt. Stringy black hair ran across his sunburned neck and over his ears. Hayes lifted his chin at the sprawling desert, clumped creosote and awkward Joshua trees undulating toward a razor-edged horizon. This was, somehow, a desolate image in front of Sam, a nostalgic moment in the present. He heard in his head, again, Hayes saying in that half-drawl, *"I'm going to kill the motherfucker."*

Sam looked down at his right hand, the topography of scar tissue like wet paper on his palm and fingers. It was Jazz who had driven him to the hospital after the accident.

The things we do to ourselves, we do them because we don't understand each other. This was how Sam felt about Hayes.

Again, he studied the firm silhouette outlined against the cabin's doorway, remembered dropping him off on base before his second tour in Afghanistan, remembered feeling angry about their conversation. And hadn't Sam thought to himself, good goddamn riddance? He had. That summer, the last Sam saw of his buddy Hayes was outside a barracks at Camp Pendleton. They had left town before sunrise. Hayes wanted to get back to base by eight that morning. He slept while Sam drove and listened to Albert King breathe hard-life lyrics through the Chevy's half-working speakers. The drive was easy, and it was a little past seven when Hayes showed his credentials to a Marine who waved them through the base's main entrance. As Sam slid the Chevy to the curb near the barracks, Hayes unbuckled his seat belt and let a long, slow exhalation of breath dramatize the moment. Sam said, "You sound like Erin when I'm washing the dishes."

"Someone needs to supervise your work."

"Believe me, I have more than enough supervision at my job. Nelson still doesn't like me. Or my work." Sam shook his head and shifted the truck into park. He left the engine running, scratched his right arm where the sun hit it through the dusty windshield. "I don't need supervision at home."

Hayes shifted in the passenger seat and glared at Sam. "There's no law that says you need to keep doing what you're doing. I'll tell you what happens. You keep walking around hating everybody and everything, you end up hating yourself. I know because it's what I did."

"And I guess you got enlightened." The spot between Sam's eyes filled with tension, and he rubbed it with thumb and index finger. "Now that you wear a uniform and keep your hair short, huh?"

Hayes bit the inside of his right cheek and peered out his window. He spoke to the parking lot, "I didn't get enlightened, Sam. I just got a chance to see things different—that was all it took for me."

"And now, after you go off and fight, you're going to come

back home and what? You're going to live in that cabin, in that place?"

"Why not?"

Sam didn't answer. He closed his eyes, tried not to think about Ryder Simms, the old man with the unkempt beard and white hair falling in tufts from beneath his green trucker's hat. He tried not to recall Ryder's gravel-shaken voice calling him a pansy, challenging his manhood. And Sam, most of all, tried not to feel the throbbing scar on his chin. He thought of the cinder-brick cabin and the surrounding desert, imagined Hayes churning soil for a small garden or trying to lay pipe for a fountain. And, in his darkest folds of thought, Sam saw Hayes plunging a shovel into white shards of bone—the bones of Ryder Simms. He sighed and scratched his face, but didn't speak.

"Besides," Hayes continued, "I'll be gone for quite a while. Who the hell knows when I'll be back? Things might change in that time. I might change in that time." He paused for a long time before adding, "I know I didn't tell you what it's like over there. I bet you're curious."

"Most people are."

A hollow laugh seeped from Hayes's throat, like a cough from a sputtering engine. "Oh, they want to know how many people you shot, what it's like to get shot at, how in the hell people look at you over there."

"I just want to know that you'll be alright, Hayes. That's all. And Erin, too."

"You want to know if I'll be safe."

"That's right."

"And I guess, if I said I would, you'd go home and feel good about everything. You'd go back to your little apartment and your wife and coming son. You'd drink coffee with cream and sugar. You'd watch a movie on Saturday night, and you'd work your shitty job with your shitty pay. You'd go back and be late on the phone bill and the electric bill. You'd visit the dentist. Shit, you'd go in for a regular checkup with your doctor and all the—"

"You got enlightened, but you got mean along with it—"

"My point," Hayes said over Sam, "is that you got a regular life and you're a regular man. You just do what's expected. That's as far as you take it. You want me to say I'm safe so you can go back to your little life and feel safe, too."

Sam sighed and shifted the Chevy into gear. "I guess it's been fun having you, buddy. I know you don't want to go back, but I need—"

"There is no such thing as safe, Sam. This is what the world is." Hayes motioned at the parking lot. "We're all soldiers, just like when we were kids. You might not like it, and you might not admit it, but we're all fighting for a piece of somebody else, something else. You can't be out of it. You can't say 'I'm not involved.' You're not safe and you never will be, okay?"

"Why keep living?"

"Your kid. For that. Stop walking around like a goddamned zombie, Sam."

"I heard you."

Hayes said, "Get out to the desert and kill something for fuck's sake."

Sam swiveled his head, pointed gun-barrel eyes at his friend Hayes, the United States Marine. "Kill something?" Sam's jaw tightened. Ryder's pale skin shaded his vision. The man sat between him and Hayes, flashed for an instant like a hologram.

Hayes nodded and said, "That's right. Get out to the desert and kill something. I mean, shoot, that's what I'm going to do."

Escaping that memory, from the darkness of the cabin, Sam walked toward the silhouette framed in the doorway. This was his best buddy, back now from some hellhole experience he couldn't describe. Back with vengeance in his head. Sam stood behind Hayes and looked beyond him to a flat spot in the center of the property. We all have our graves, Sam knew. It's just some of us get buried a little before we mean to, shallow and early. The thought disgusted him, made him feel dirty. "You mean what you said, about Jazz?"

Without turning around, Hayes said, "You know I do what I say."

"Why'd you get out of the Corps, Hayes?"

Two short coughs came from deep in Hayes's belly. He shook with their violence and cleared his throat, huffed out a cloud of frozen breath. "I lost my patience with stupid questions. Shit, I lost patience with all kinds of questions." Hayes swung his gaze eastward and yawned. "I had my share of the world, that's all. I'm just sick of the whole thing."

"Like the rest of us."

A haunted laugh burned from Hayes, and he turned to look at Sam.

Sam's knees went rubber, and he clenched the muscles in his stomach, tried to stop the flip-flop of nerves where his sternum met his belly.

"I'm sorry I haven't been down to see your family, Sam. You know, I got home and I had things to take care of."

"You don't need to apologize to me, buddy."

"I called my uncle in Reno, wanted to see if I could find my old man. You know, I can't tell you what it is. There's something off about him running out on this place. Anyway, I get in touch up there, and my uncle says he hasn't heard from the man in a year. Can you believe that?" Sam's eyes darted, for a brief instant, to the spot of cold dirt beyond Hayes. "I said, can you believe that?"

Sam shook his head. "It's a surprise."

Hayes lifted the shotgun, pointed it casually at Sam. "That's what I said myself. It's a surprise. I said, 'That's a surprise, Uncle. You sure you haven't heard from the man?' And my uncle cursed at me and said, 'Not so much as a letter asking for more money.' What I did is, I called some places around Reno, places I knew the old man to have some fondness for. Strip clubs, mostly. And, you know, not one person at any of those fine establishments had seen Ryder Simms. He hadn't been to Reno. Not as far as I could find."

"You ask here in town?"

The shotgun probed at the air. "There's an idea. You and me always were on the same page. See, I was going to do that next. I wanted to find this other son of a gun first, but I could go ask around about my old man. That's an idea." Hayes turned and took the porch steps down before plodding across the weed-filled yard. He swung the shotgun like a metal detector.

Sam followed him outside, hunched into his coat against the stiff cold. "It's cold as shit out here, Hayes."

"I want to show you something."

Sam stepped off the porch and fell in beside Hayes as they moved toward the center of the property. This wasn't good. Sam's fear and guilt became bile in his mouth. His stomach flipped and dropped into his ass. *You're going to get that shotgun in your face,* he thought. *This is not the same Hayes you dropped off at Camp Pendleton, no sir. This son of a gun is the real deal, and he's got some kind of deep anger inside him.*

"I like to hike around here, up in those hills," Hayes said, and pointed with the shotgun. "I was thinking, too, I might like to get myself a dog."

"Oh, yeah?"

"Say," Hayes said, "did I ever tell you about the war dogs, Sam?"

Sam didn't answer. They moved to the center of the property, the wide dirt lot framed by desert brush, and Hayes planted his booted feet. Sam's ass dropped still further, seemed to reach the backsides of his calves. *This is what it feels like,* he thought, *to jump off a bridge and plunge straight to hell.*

"Look at this dirt," Hayes said. "You see how it's a little too regular all around? Like it's been patted down?"

"I don't know what you mean."

"Like it's been dug up and put back, that's how it looks."

Sam said, "So what?"

"My old man buried something out here, that's what. I wonder what it is?"

"Maybe he shot a coyote, or maybe he buried a couple of

those cats that used to run around here. I remember that gray one with the bent leg."

"Yeah," Hayes agreed. "Sally isn't around—I bet she's dead." He turned and squinted at the cabin. His mouth curled, and he turned back to the spot in the dirt. "We used to bury dead things at the north end of the property, though. I can't see why he'd switch that, start to bury things out here."

"He was nuts," Sam tried, and walked past Hayes with measured nonchalance. He angled toward the line of desert with his hands in his coat. After a few steps, he turned and stared at Hayes. "I guess you shouldn't dig up anything to do with your dad, Hayes. If it's buried, hell, it should stay buried, don't you think?"

Hayes squinted at Sam, ran his tongue along the roof of his mouth, and let his head fall to one shoulder. After his thoughts ran their course, Hayes straightened and looked off toward the heightening sun. His shadow fell askew to the rear and made his stance look off-kilter and haunting. Hayes shook his head slightly and said, "If it's buried, I doubt I want to dig it up. Tell you what, though, all this talk about strip clubs makes me thirsty. You mind driving with me into town? I want to do a little detective work, and I could use a sidekick."

Before Everything

Sam scraped his arms and belly while crawling along the desert's dirt floor. He winced as tiny cholla spines caught on his shirt and socks. He stopped to pull them out one by one, listened for the delicate crunch of Hayes moving toward him. The sun had settled low over the horizon, and Sam was holding out until dusk fell—he wanted to make Hayes piss his pants, scare the hell out of him. But Hayes was quiet, stealthy. Hayes knew how to stalk a person. And that was how Sam felt, as if he were being stalked. He thought: *I shouldn't always be afraid, dammit. I need him to be afraid. Him. Not me.* Sam peered through the desert brush—dry creosote and scattered juniper, strong-scented desert shrub—and tried to spot Hayes moving sentry-like toward him.

But no. Hayes was a ghost.

Where in the hell was that boy?

Sam dug an elbow into the ground, pushed himself into a kneeling position. His two-by-four sat harmless in front of him. He squinted into the falling sun, just low enough to obscure his vision. Hayes could—if he wanted—take advantage of that and approach fast, raise his two-by-four and shout "Gotcha, you son of a gun!" Sam lowered his head, swiveled from side to side in search of a shadow or sudden movement. After Ryder had driven away, a dust cloud rising behind the truck and whirling skyward, Sam had hidden in a dry gully, watched Hayes look for him. Sam noticed how he moved with exact precision, angling first one direction and then the next, as if sketching a grid in the desert. When he didn't find Sam, Hayes began to circle.

That was when Sam started to change position, to huddle for a few minutes behind a bush or boulder and, when Hayes turned, to dart for cover elsewhere. He kept moving as long as he could, but now Sam was tired. He wanted to catch Hayes off-guard.

But first, Sam had to find his friend.

Sam crawled a few feet to his left, dragged the two-by-four along beside him. When he looked again at the sprawling desert, he caught a glint from his mom's trailer. The door was open, and his mom stood there with a hand over her eyes.

After a delay, she called to him, "Sam! You better come home for dinner! It's getting dark out here!"

I can't answer her, he thought, *or Hayes will find me.*

Again, tinged with anger, she called: "You better get your asses back here, or I'm going to whip you, Sam! Answer me, dammit!"

Sam clenched the two-by-four. *One shout,* he thought. *Fast, and I'll move to the left, circle back, and find Hayes.* He stood as if being lifted by an elevator. His left knee cracked. *Okay, I'll say we're on our way back—she'll leave us alone for a bit.* Sam cleared his throat and screamed, "We'll be back in a few minutes!"

Now, he thought, *I have to move.*

Sam bent at his knees, swiveled left, darted around a thick-branched juniper. When he came around the tree—it was taller than him—he caught slight movement in the sunlight, but he was moving fast across the desert and couldn't stop. In his head, he was reciting a mantra: *Change position. Take cover. Change position. Take cover.* His eyes were on his feet, on the slight indentations he was making in the dirt.

He didn't see Hayes—or the odd, menacing jut of the two-by-four—until it prodded him in the chest. Sam was yanked upright by the sharp pain against his skin. His eyes shot to Hayes, his friend's angular face half-shadowed in the pre-dusk light. Sam's stomach dropped and he yelped, fell back into the dirt with a hard exhalation of breath. As he fell, he dropped his two-by-four. Sam sprawled—looking up at Hayes—as if he were an iguana frozen in fear.

Hayes lowered the point of the two-by-four to aim at Sam's head. He said, "Looks like I got you, sucker." One side of his mouth curled upward, toyed with a smug grin. "I win, Sam. I win again."

Flat on his back, in the dirt and scattered cholla, Sam groaned and said, "I don't know why it is I always run. Whenever I play with you, no matter what I do, I wind up dead."

9

"I'll drive us like the old days. Fast and loose." Hayes walked toward the cabin, said over his shoulder, "You want to help me change this tire?" The shotgun pointed at the Dodge Dart, gray and silent as a tombstone.

"Nope, but I don't mind waiting." Sam turned and followed Hayes toward the car. He wondered about ways to get out of this: *I can say I have to get back to Erin and Reagan, or that it's my only day off.* But Hayes, like he always did, pulled at Sam, kept him lashed to actions he couldn't end. Why was that? Why was it that friends from childhood and onward could pull us into storms of hardship and hell and wonder. *This, Sam reminded himself, is what friendship is—it's living in the storm, even when you don't want to.*

"You're still lazy, huh?" Hayes glared back at Sam but kept on toward the car. When he reached it, he set the shotgun on the hood. He walked behind the Dodge and reappeared rolling a spare tire toward Sam. "Let a man do all the real work, is that it?"

Sam reached the car, leaned against the front fender and watched Hayes as he began to twist the lugs with a grease-stained tire iron. "You're a big boy. And believe me when I say: I do enough hard work five days a week."

"I was kidding, Sam."

"It didn't sound like it."

Hayes stopped what he was doing and gazed at Sam. "You have something you're upset about, buddy? Something you want to tell me?"

Sam saw gray cloud cover reflected in Hayes's eyes. "You mean besides this talk about killing Jazz?" Sam couldn't understand how, after saying what he did, Hayes sounded normal, like a good old boy back from a trip. "I shouldn't be upset about that?"

"You can be upset about a job when it needs doing, but it still needs to get done. That's how it works over there, and it's how it works over here. You don't like it, well, then you don't—"

"It's about what's right." Sam set his jaw, ran a hand over the back of his neck. "What do you have against Jazz?" *Now,* Sam thought, *we'll talk about that morning eight years ago—that's what this is. It can't be anything else. Can it?*

Hayes went back to the tire iron, ripped through the lugs and spun them off like a dentist pulling loose teeth. "Let's just say, I need to take my anger out on someone, and he happens to be the one."

"It's not that simple. This is about what happened outside John's Place. You know it. I know it. The whole town knows it. And now, now that you're some kind of war hero, you need to go back and make Jazz pay for that—am I right?"

Hayes loosed a maniacal, cackling, indifferent laugh. "You think—" He covered his mouth with a greasy hand and dropped it when he had himself under control. "You think I care about that? Oh, man. You really have me under a microscope, Sam. I'm so immature I care about a grown man choking me out when I was a smart-ass teenager. Okay, pal. Sure."

"What is it?" Sam crossed his arms, sensed the lie bubbling up through Hayes's throat. And, at the same time, a question ran through him: *What happened with Ryder, was that any better than what Hayes is talking about doing to Jazz? Maybe,* Sam thought, *the two of us are meant to hurt the world. Maybe we're meant to leave it worse than when we entered it.*

Stop, he begged himself. *Stop thinking about it.*

Hayes said, "This is about sending kids out, sending them somewhere else. That's what it's about, Sam. Asking kids to do a thing, something they shouldn't have to do. That's all it's ever about."

"What kids?"

"You and me, okay? Dammit, Sam. Me. It's about sending me away for a reason I can't name. It's about the way it all is, this—" Hayes waved an arm at the sky, shook his head. "It's about the shit. And how *hero* is just another way to say *shit*, but with different letters." Hayes went back to the tire, began to hoist the chassis with a lift.

Sam pushed away from the car, ambled into the yard. He studied the sky for a long moment. "You think it'll snow, like they say?" He didn't want to talk about Jazz anymore. Or killing. Or heroes who called themselves shit and kept wanting to talk about killing and more shit.

Behind him, Hayes said, "If it doesn't snow today, it'll rain tomorrow. That's how it always works. You get half of what they promise, and it always comes too damn late."

Sam stared at the sky. He wanted snow—white, cold, pure, endless snow.

He wanted to wipe the world clean. He wanted the blankest of slates. The closest to erasure he could get was moving back through time.

In his mind, he arrived at the day when Ryder had pistol-whipped him. He saw the Luger. And felt the constant ache of his jaw and head. Soon after Hayes had dragged Sam out of the cabin and retrieved the Luger, they stopped at a liquor store and bought some cheap whiskey. One benefit of being a teenager in Bumfuck, America. And then they were parked alongside a square white building with the word COCKTAILS spray-painted in green across the side. A single neon beer sign blinked in a dark window. Three old pickups and a rusty Ford Probe waited outside in the dirt lot.

Hayes clambered from his seat and slammed the door. He stumbled toward the entrance. Hayes could hold his drink—that wasn't the problem. Nope. The problem was, Sam knew, that Ryder Simms was leering over Hayes like the world's largest and darkest shadow. As they neared high school graduation, both Sam and Hayes craved a freedom they couldn't find in their small town, and Ryder was a massive black hole in Hayes's life, a force greater than gravity pulling him harder and harder toward its savage evil.

Sam felt the dried blood along his jaw. It ran in a crooked line. He winced at his own touch. Again, murder emerged in his thoughts—he imagined himself pointing the Luger at Ryder, pointing it straight at his black, throbbing heart. What was it Ryder had said to him? *It'll stop your heart if it hits you in the right spot.*

Sam watched as Hayes found the bar's front door. He opened the door to the white building, collected himself, and stumbled across the threshold. *Hayes*, Sam thought, *I better keep you company, buddy.*

The first thing Sam noticed was a smell like chicken boiled far too long—a mad smell, an odor that ran in through his nose and penetrated his mind. *It's the smell of years rolled up and wasted in a bar, that's what it is.* Scattered in a row of booths were some regulars. They had that washed-up look that attaches itself to barflies: dirty Levi's, scuffed boots, and a puffy look that ran up their necks and into their faces. The guy closest to the door twisted his head toward Sam. Stringy hair flapped across his chin and one eye closed as he stared and said, "Never seen you before."

Sam puffed his chest, tried for good posture. "Passing through. Just need to piss."

"Make it quick."

"I wouldn't want to stay," Sam said, and tossed his gaze around the place. The light was dim and confined to the corners. Scattered neon beer signs hung on the walls, but none were lit. The thin carpet was covered with splotches of spilled alcohol. *This is a place to drink*, Sam thought, *pure and simple.* Ahead of him, Hayes was draped across the bar, half tilted on a wobbly stool. Sam wandered over and lifted a hand at the bartender. "Can I have a beer?"

"You ain't old enough," the bartender said.

"That stops you?" Sam watched the man carefully. Age restrictions didn't matter this far out in the desert. He knew that and so did the bartender. "One beer is all. I can handle that."

A brown bottle appeared on the bar. The bartender, in a loose-fitting flannel and torn Levi's, glared at Hayes, but spoke to Sam. "You can have a beer, but none for him. One beer and you're gone—that's all."

Sam nodded, slid a five-dollar bill to the man before he drifted back to a dark corner and crossed his arms over his chest. Sam sat next to Hayes and swallowed warm beer. "This place is horrible," he said. "And the beer is warm."

"I decided," Hayes said. His head swung toward Sam, hung limp against a shoulder. "I figured it out."

"What?"

"The Marine Corps. I figured it out."

Sam waited.

"I'm going to join up," Hayes said. "That's exactly what I'm going to do."

"The hell you are. You hate jarheads." Sam saw Jazz again, the recruiter, choking Hayes in the parking lot at John's Place. He saw Jazz lay Hayes, unconscious and defenseless, softly on the pavement. Sam said, "And you hate Jazz."

"Can't fight it, Sam. I can't fight what's pulling me anymore. You're looking at the newest Marine Corps recruit. That's me."

Sam sipped more beer, tried a vague, absent-minded smile.

"A killer, Sam. You're looking at a killer."

"I'm not sure Jazz likes you, buddy. You think he'll have you?"

Hayes said, "I can find a way past that. You think he cares about what I said? You saw him. He dropped his card right on the table that morning at the diner. The way I talked to him, something like that, it practically makes me a number one recruit. They like a little mean in their boys. You know it. Jazz knows it. And I know it."

"You had too much today, Hayes. Look, I'm fine." Sam slapped himself with one hand, grimaced in pain. "See, my jaw doesn't even hurt. No need for guilt or anything like that. You see, the two of us, we'll be alright."

Hayes shook his head, said nothing. His lips moved against themselves. "My daddy's going to make me a nothing, Sam. That's if I stay around here, and I know that for a fact."

Sam contemplated his beer, tried to think of something to say.

A voice came from behind them: "I thought I told you to piss and leave?"

The man with the stringy hair carried a bone-handled hunting knife and too much weight in his belly. He was a tall man—too tall. He was a giant, an abnormal organism, a horrid sight with his scuffed cowboy boots and bony hands. "I guess you don't listen very good," he said.

Sam stared at him through the dim light and beer-smelling air, this long-legged spider with a round, bulbous torso pressed against a denim shirt. Sam tried to catch himself, but a word flew from his lips: "Freak."

A hush ran through the bar. "What did you say to me?"

"He said, you're a freak." Hayes pushed to his elbows, lurched from the bar stool, and found the strength and balance to turn and face the giant. "You're a freak." The word came out like spittle. Hayes steadied himself, laced his hands behind his head, and grinned. "Nobody likes a freak, now do they?"

No, Sam thought, *nobody likes a freak. And, hell, nobody likes to be called a freak, now do they?* Sam inched toward the door, tried to will the giant into submission. But he knew from the vibrations in his chest that things would not be calm or okay or simple. No, not in a place like this. Not with Hayes in the bag and knocking toward insanity. If one pistol-whipping wasn't enough, Sam had no words for how to get through this day—if only he had the Luger.

That would end this before it started.

The giant stepped toward Sam, let his left arm—it was skinny and gnarled like a tree limb—grasp for purchase. His hand closed around Sam's neck, squeezed. The giant's face clenched. Sweat ran between his eyes and across his chin. A short, rough sound left his throat, punched Sam in the face. "You punk bastard. Who you think—"

Like opening a door to winter, Sam could breathe again.

The giant collapsed, howled skyward, and reached for his right knee.

Hayes lifted his booted foot, slammed it into the giant's knee again. While he twisted his boot back and forth atop the man's kneecap, Hayes grinned at the regulars in the bar, swung his head from left to right like a politician sweeping the room.

"Jesus, Hayes—let him up." Sam backed toward the door, tried to shut out the giant's low-pitched moans. The sounds echoed in the bar, reminded Sam of running through a tunnel or going down into an old desert mine.

"He wanted to make you hurt, Sam. Didn't you, big boy?" Hayes leaned over, planted his face above the giant's. The room shrank as people closed in on the two men. And that's what Hayes was... With this lone violent act, he became a man. Hayes pressed harder into the knee. Groans pushed through the giant's throat. "I know, this hurts, doesn't it? It hurts like hell and that's all it's ever going to do. It'll hurt forever." Hayes lifted his foot, drove it down with sledgehammer force.

The giant fainted. Hayes shrugged, lifted his head and scanned the crowd.

"Hayes? Now, okay?" Sam pushed through the door and lunged into desert air, soft night air lush with the scent of creosote. He jogged toward the Dodge and, as Hayes stumbled behind him, fell into the driver's seat. The engine sounded distant as he started the car and shifted into drive. Hayes took the passenger seat, and they shot toward the highway—half in shadow, the angry bartender hovered outside the bar. He crossed his arms over his chest and watched them with off-white eyes. Sam kept his eyes on the road, tried to outrun the headlights and their imperfect pendulum arc.

»»»»»

Later, atop a fire access road, the desert sprawled below:

"It's somewhere to go, that's all. It's something to do."

"You got right here, buddy. This town, we know you. I know you."

"I need to get away from my dad."

"You put that big man on his ass, the one in the bar."

"So what?"

"Are you telling me you can't put your dad on his ass?"

"I'll put you on your ass."

"You got nothing to prove to me. I'm just here—that's all for me."

"So there's nothing else?"

"Besides what?"

"Besides this fucking shit town, man!"

"There's lots. There's holidays and Fourth of July. Thanksgiving. There's girls who want you to put your arms around them. Beer. Whiskey. There's girls. Lots of girls."

"Man, I can name the beautiful girls on one hand."

"I never said those are the ones that want you."

"You make my point for me."

"Hayes, think about this before you do it."

"There's places besides here. Other places you can live, think about. Things to eat and drink. People, there's people all over this world."

"You sound like you've thought this through."

"You know what I'm saying, Sam. I know you do. Don't admit it. That's fine with me, but don't hold it against me that I'm more than this. I mean... This cannot be all there is—it just can't. I swear, I won't let that be the truth."

"You're going to forget this, forget me."

"No, Sam. What I want is to forget my dad. I want to kill that man because he won't die. He will never die. I know it'll be pain, nothing but pain, if I don't leave."

"You hate the Marine Corps."

"I hate that man more than anything. I always will."

10

Love was an easy word to say, but—my god, Sam thought—it was the hardest word to mean. He lifted his mangled hand and stared at it. Wrinkles and charred terrain, bungled nerve endings and collapsed pores. Lost paths and ravines. All the landscapes of the heart right there on his palm. Sam shivered with the cold, turned to watch as Hayes lifted the flat tire off the hub and rolled it aside. He lifted the replacement, set it where it belonged, made an adjustment or two. He stood slowly and slapped his hands together, brushed the dirt off them. "These knees keep killing me. It gets worse every single day."

"I guess they did make you an old man." Sam walked to the tire, bent to one knee, and began to tighten the lugs by hand. "I guess I can help, now that you got the hard stuff done."

"You think I didn't mean it, what I said."

Sam finished tightening each lug and paused. He turned and looked up at Hayes. His face gleamed with gray, and a firm line stretched from the middle of his brow down to his crooked nose. Without smiling, Sam said, "I think you *think* you mean it, but you don't want to mean it. If you did—"

"I would have never told you." Hayes put both hands on his hips and sighed. He looked away from Sam, toward collapsed cloud cover. A distant shard of light blue spread to the north. "You think maybe I wanted you to talk me out of it. You think—I just bet you think—that I'm crazy as hell. Hayes, the war hero. Back from battle and crazy as hell. Hayes, the good old small-town kid with stripes on his sleeve and medals on his chest. Why would he go and do a thing like this, kill a fellow Marine, a brother in arms?"

"You got it." Sam stood, watched Hayes stare into distant nothing.

"Maybe I wanted you along for the ride, Sam. Maybe I just—"

"I got a wife. I got a kid. I can't get mixed up in your wild plans."

Hayes crossed his arms, swung his sharp profile back on Sam.

Sam again felt his stomach drop. He imagined a bag of coins gone loose in a child's hand. *I don't know why I keep feeling that.* Sam knew Hayes wouldn't kill him. Or, he thought he knew. And pointing that shotgun at him was like jabbing a finger. No more and no less, though it felt like more. Behind Hayes, Sam could see the two chest-high piles of sandbags. Why not, as humans, fortify our positions—didn't we have something to protect, to defend? Sam knew that he had something to protect and defend: A wife. A son. Little more than that. But little is more than none, and most men, he tried to convince himself, labored for less. There came that word again—*love*—and Sam sensed its shape on his tongue. Fine, then. Love was all he had to protect and to defend, but that should be enough. Small, maybe. But enough.

"You, Sam, are more mixed up than any man I've ever met."

"It's easy to feel right with a gun in your hand, isn't it?"

Hayes glanced over Sam's shoulder at the shotgun resting on the Dodge's hood. He brushed by Sam, hefted it, and rested the barrel on his shoulder. "Let's see here." He lowered the gun, traced his vision along the barrel, to the stock, back up the long, deadly form. "You know what? It is easier to feel right with a gun in hand. Dammit, you are right on the money with that, Sam. How'd you go and get so wise? You been taking a class I don't know about?"

Sam shook his head. "Talk about everything like it's a joke."

"It is, except for when it's not. How's that for a punch line?" Hayes rested the shotgun against his shoulder again and breathed deeply of the cold, still air. "Are you going to finish up with that tire, or you want a real man to do it?"

A real man? What in the hell was that?

Maybe it meant the willingness to die for something. Or the endurance to work for something of little value. Or maybe it was about doing things you didn't like because there were so few other ways forward. Once he'd started working at John's Place, Sam had found things he didn't like to do. Carrying out the heavy, grease-dripping black trash bags was one. Scrubbing the flat-top grill with a wire brush at the end of his shift was another. Come to think of it, he didn't like much about the job. Every so often, Sam caught himself taking pleasure in sliding a perfect pair of over-easy eggs onto a clean white plate. This—on most days—was the height of his pleasures. About three months into his job at the diner, Sam noticed the fried-fish smell lingered wherever he went in town. Took him a bit to reason this out, but one day he realized: *That smell is me.*

A man smells like his work, Sam learned—that's how it is.

And still, he went back for the late shift that ran until midnight. Back to the ring of fork tines on cheap plates, the rattle of coffee spoons in near-dirty mugs. Back to a waitress called Nora, who smelled like cigarettes and told him once a week how she was on her third decade at the diner. Back to ten dollars an hour and a grimace on his face, one he couldn't shake if he tried. Back to Nelson and his ceaseless bitching.

The boy was the reason—the one who slept in Sam's apartment like a little alien. That boy, the one who cried when his mom ripped the tit away, and who followed Sam's eyes with his own. The boy who'd grown so much before Sam's eyes. Sam fried eggs eight hours a day for one Reagan Hayes Carl. Sam spent most of his days trying not to be afraid of the boy. This fear was a thing he failed to understand, but not understanding a thing inside himself wasn't new to Sam.

Needing money, that he understood.

And Sam and Erin (and the growing boy) needed the money.

Unlike Hayes—over in the war wearing body armor and carrying a gun—an apron was Sam's uniform, and a spatula was his weapon.

Thinking about all this was how Sam had marred his right hand on a clear Saturday afternoon, an afternoon when the pleasant odor of sage drifted across the desert highway and, as customers entered, licked at the diner's grease-flecked interior. Nine hamburger patties sizzled on the grill. Sam lifted one and flipped it with casual expertise. He readied plates in front of the grill. Sam toasted sesame buns and arranged lettuce, tomato, and onion slices like fine adornments. The hamburger: still a top seller in small-town America. Sam shrugged. *What the hell? People want their meat, and they want it fast.* As he turned another burger, Sam heard the diner's doorbell chime. He heard a man sit down at the counter, directly across from the grill, but did not imagine he'd see Jazz that late in the day.

Jazz was a breakfast man, a coffee and pancake man.

But when Sam turned from the grill to grab a few more plates, he found Jazz's stark blue eyes prying into him. Sam said, "Mr. Gung Ho himself, I never see you when I work the afternoon." Ever since Hayes had shipped out again, a lump rose in Sam's throat whenever he saw Jazz. Shoot, he felt his stomach twist when he saw Jazz's truck outside Jelly Donut, or when he heard that big V-8 roar past on the highway—no, Sam had nothing against Jazz. It was Hayes, is what it was—Jazz made Sam think of his buddy.

"Thought I'd come by and see you, partner." Jazz rubbed a finger along his crisp collar, dropped both hands to rest on the countertop. His thumbs rubbed slowly against his index fingers.

Sam lifted a stack of plates from beneath the counter and, while he arranged them next to the grill, said, "No idea what you want with me—I'm just a short-order cook making ten an hour. You, though, you're big time around here. You have an important job to do, don't you?" He flipped two more patties, turned back to Jazz and let a short-lived smile flash across his face.

Be pleasant, Sam thought, *it's your job.*

Jazz flexed the fist-like muscles in his cheeks. His face shone bright, smooth as a wooden axe handle. "Thing is, I heard your buddy is making quite the hero out of himself."

"You heard from him?" Sam felt the blood thicken in his veins. His breath caught in his throat. There'd been no word from

Hayes in a long time.

"No, no. Not directly. I just got word through the grapevine. Ran into a Marine back stateside, guy I know. He said he ran into Hayes, that he was glad to know a guy from his same town, you know?"

"Where was this?" Sam moved toward the counter. His chest pounded every time he thought about the war. He couldn't help seeing visions of Hayes coming home in a coffin, a flag draped over it. He avoided the newspapers and cable television. He'd written to Hayes, half-joking emails asking for any news about coming home. And he'd sent a couple packages, boxes with some paperbacks and candy. You don't hear back, though, and you start to think: *What the hell?* He knew Hayes wasn't dead—he'd have heard about that. Too much small-town gossip in John's Place for news of a dead Marine to be avoided.

"In-country, man, where else? These suckers are the boots on the ground you're reading about. These Marines are the tit's nipples. That's how it works. You'll get a kick out of what the guy tells me: He says Hayes is a real Rambo-type or something. That they were in this town—real kind of shitty place with people living in shacks and there's no running water—and they needed to get in this house. Well, they got the bush-league trainees with them. Not Americans or Brits, not the French, neither. These are the ones they're training to be in it for themselves, you know?

"So, it's Hayes who says, 'You dumbfucks go in first—kick down that door and get the fuck in there.' Well, according to this guy came back, the newbies won't do it, you know? Hayes shoves his weapon in their faces, but they won't budge. Scared little fuckers, I guess. So, what he does, is he picks one of the guys up and throws the fucker through the door—like the Hulk or Batman or some shit. Well, the door goes down like you'd think and the newbie lands on his back."

Sam's chest expanded, contracted, rippled against the grease-stained apron draped from his neck. He opened his mouth and tried to take in more air. His breathing got this way, and he didn't know how to stop it. He lifted a hand to the nape of his neck and rubbed, tried to direct his attention away from the futile pounding of his heart.

Jazz continued, "And the fucker starts screaming his head off—as if bin-fucking-Laden has a bazooka pointed right at his little pecker. You know, he's still scared, right? Well, it's your boy Hayes who goes inside first—not a damn question asked. He lets a few rounds go and drags out some towel-head son of a bitch with a World War II pistol lodged in his waistband. Extremist, this guy tells me. Inside the house, they find a case of grenades, a few dozen assault weapons, and enough explosives to blow their asses into hell. You believe that? Your boy, your buddy, out there kicking ass and taking names. It's really something to hear that, I can tell you. You remember what he was? Shoot, now he's on top of the world. With a weapon in his hands, too."

Sam pressed his teeth together, let off when pain started in his jaw. "He kill the guy?" The question pressed through his lips like paper through a straw. *Air*, he thought, *is scarce right this second.*

"The newbie? No, no way. That ain't allowed because—"

"The other guy, I meant."

"The towel-head? Shit..." Jazz bit his bottom lip, scratched behind one ear. "I got no idea. Forgot to ask. Who gives a shit?"

Sam turned back to the sizzling grill. He heard grease popping beneath the burger patties and the soft tinkle of silverware in the diner. He heard the chirp of Jazz's lips as he called out to the waitress. He heard other things, too—the mousy voice of Erin calling to him from the bathroom in their apartment, Hayes laughing at him in the Dodge's driver's seat, gunfire echoing down the throat of some desert canyon, a little boy howling from the confines of a crib, the dumbfounding crack of the Luger against his own chin. The pressure in his chest built and released, like a balloon filled with water and then punctured. The warmth came, a pleasant burn that filtered through his chest and into his arms. His fingers tingled. Sam tilted, wavered, caught himself with a short step. But he couldn't hold his balance. Why, he wondered, had someone turned out the lights in the diner? It was dark wherever he pointed his eyes, and the blackness pooled around him, whirled against the edges of his vision. *Circles, those are dark circles, and they're coming for me.* He lost feeling in his right leg. He began to tilt, list, spin.

From close behind him, Sam heard Jazz's voice:

"Hey, buddy," he said, "the hell are you doing over there?"

Sam closed his eyes and lowered his right hand toward the sizzling grill. He couldn't stop himself—his strength was gone. He toppled forward and, without fear or care or worry, pressed his right hand onto the grill's hot steel.

»»»»»

Sam had a feeling that he was awake, but he was lost somewhere inside his own head. A fog held his thoughts, seemed thick and full inside him. There were smells—he couldn't name them. A soft clink beside his head. Slight pressure below his elbow, like somebody pinching a numb hand attached to his shoulder. His thoughts were simple: *What is this? Where am I? Who brought me here?*

Why?

All questions, but no answers.

Voices entered his head as if small and distant.

— Yes, there.

— Thank you.

— See, here? This is the place.

— Can we begin to wrap the procedure?

— When you're ready, doctor.

— Almost. He'll be fine. In pain, maybe. But fine.

Sam tried to push his consciousness to the surface above the fog, tried to force himself from semi-sleep, but a moment came when he lost the desire. He settled into the fog, descended, drifted back to darkness.

»»»»

"I never saw anything like it."

"Did he say anything?"

"No—I told him the story about Hayes, about the war, and he just—"

"You don't have to say it."

"I never saw anything like it."

"You said that already."

»»»»

"Sam?"

He knew the voice. It was Erin. He opened his eyes, saw a small gray-lit window in one corner, a wooden chair near a beige wall. Closer, a blurred figure that cleared after a moment. It was her. Blonde hair and a slight nose, a small woman folded into a chair with a tiny mass huddled in a blue blanket between her arms—that was Sam's son in there. All at once, he felt shame burn in his stomach and spread into his throat. He wanted to vomit but forced himself to breathe through his mouth. "What the hell happened, Erin?"

"You had an accident at work."

Sam shifted in the hospital bed, tried to bring his elbows beneath him.

"Don't move too much. They said you can go home when the anesthesia wears off, once you can walk on your own. They don't want you hanging on to me." She paused and, after clearing her throat, said, "Because of the baby."

Sam wasn't in pain, but there were small twitches below his shoulder. And he remembered. He remembered the story booming from Jazz's mouth, the stark vision of Hayes darting into a house in some far-off country. He remembered the sizzle of the beef on the flat-top grill and lowering his hand. And he remembered a sensation like hot water below his elbow, a fierce scream rattling from his throat. Sam said, "They called an ambulance?"

"Nope. Jazz took you here. Said he had to carry you, that you screamed your head off the whole way here."

Sam did not remember.

"What happened with you, Sam?"

"I can't remember."

Erin stood over him, touched his forehead with one hand. She bounced slightly with the baby. Reagan shifted in her arms. "Are you okay?"

"You tell me."

"Your hand won't be too pretty after it heals, but the doctor says you'll be fine. They didn't need to do any skin grafts. You're lucky—they take it from your ass if they need it." Erin smiled at him and rubbed a hand over the boy's head.

Sam reached out and touched her arm, moved his good hand to his son. "Let me see him."

Erin folded the blanket back over Reagan's head, and Sam saw his son's smooth white face. His eyes were closed, and his nostrils moved in and out with his breath.

"How's he been?"

Erin lifted her eyebrows. "He's tired, Sam. And so am I."

"I'm sorry. I don't know what happened. The last thing I remember, I was making burgers, one for Jazz, and I just—"

"Don't, Sam. I'm just glad you're okay. You scared the hell out of me."

"What did Jazz tell you?"

Erin shifted on the balls of her feet and sank into the wooden chair beside his bed. "He wouldn't say anything about Hayes, if that's what you want to know. Mostly, he just kept saying he'd never seen anything like it. I thought he was a soldier."

"He's no soldier."

"I don't want to talk about him."

Sam felt the drugs wearing away, and he managed to prop himself higher on his pillow. He squinted at Erin, tried to read into her expression. There was nothing. No anger or sadness or fear. She looked... tired.

She blew a lock of hair from her eyes, leaned back and stared at the ceiling tiles. "I feel like I've been dragged through a keyhole."

"I'm sorry, Erin. This is trouble we don't need."

"Yeah."

"I need to get a new job, something where I'm out in the world. Not trapped in a kitchen." Sam smiled as he said it, tried to push away the shame wrapping itself around his heart. "I get too pent up, Erin."

Erin shook her head. With her free hand, she rubbed the side of her face. "You're on night-feeding duty, you bastard... after this. I deserve to sleep in, especially if you'll be at home for a while."

Sam lifted his right hand. It was wrapped in white bandages and hung in front of him like a huge, soft hammer. "I hope I can work like this."

"Well, we know one thing you won't be doing." Erin lifted her eyebrows at him. A smile lurked at the corner of her mouth. "Just so we're clear."

"Right," Sam said, "no video games. No washing dishes. I have a tough go ahead of me. What a bummer."

Erin's smile spread, lit her entire face. "I'm so freaking sick of you."

"You love me so much," Sam said, "it's pathetic."

11

"When's the last time you were here?"

Sam rolled his eyes and stared out the Dodge's fly-splattered windshield at Irma's Road Stop. It was a strip club and bar in a flat square building with corrugated-metal siding. Just off the highway, the dirt parking lot was half full with pickup trucks and motorcycles. Sam didn't want to tell Hayes the truth: He'd been to Irma's with Jazz a few times, watched the man toss dollar bills onto the stage like they didn't matter. He'd stopped meeting Jazz here when Erin found out—not like Sam wanted to watch strippers bend and shake, but Jazz had dragged him to Irma's one night and, for a few weeks, he'd gotten home late on weekdays. Talk about an ultimatum. When Erin found out, she didn't speak to him for two days, left him eating toast for dinner. Sam grunted and decided: He lied to Hayes, "The last time I took you. Right before you went back east. I think it was your first tour."

Hayes chuckled. Nostalgia came through what he said next. "Right, that was a hell of a night. The night before you and Erin got married, wasn't it? Didn't you two go down—"

"To the courthouse. The very next day. I'll never forget it because I was hungover for my own damn wedding."

"I was hungover for my plane ride to North Carolina."

Sam laughed as he said, "Try to explain a hangover to your bride, and that's after you make it clear the courthouse is how you're getting it done." Sam looked down at the silver band on his finger. He remembered that day in detail, how Erin had clung to him. He'd said, "Are you ready, Mrs. Carl?" They were both nervous. His stomach twisted in on itself. Part nerves and part alcohol. Ahead, the county clerk's office leered at them, a flat, two-story face with wide windows for eyes.

"I'm ready, Mr. Carl," Erin said. "Does it look like it's staring us down?"

"What? The future?"

Erin had grinned and said, "The building, smart-ass."

Sam tapped his pockets, came up empty. "Do you have your checkbook?"

Erin nodded and lifted her purple pocketbook. "I have it right here, and I even think the check will clear."

"Okay. I'm ready if you are."

"Waiting on you, Mr. Carl."

They'd moved down the winding, concrete pathway through manicured cacti and stonework—the building doubled as headquarters for the sheriff's department, human services, and a host of other public offices. Sam had never been to the place, and it had an official look to it, like a building you'd only visit if you were in some kind of trouble. He reminded himself that they weren't in trouble, but rather headed deeper into adulthood. *This is what it means to grow up,* he told himself, *you make decisions and choose directions, and the world lets you know—someday, somehow—whether you did things the right way.*

As they pushed through the glass front doors into the air-conditioned lobby, Sam sensed their hold on their life as children slipping away like clouds after a brief storm. And as they approached the office door, slightly ajar with a stenciled County Clerk label, Sam turned to Erin, traced her profile with his vision. *How will she change? And me, how will I change? What will we be in five years, ten, twenty? Wait a minute—who and what are we now?* These questions had flashed through him like rapid gunfire, perforated every cell in his body. *I don't know who we are, and neither does she. But here we go. Here we go.*

Sam heard the phrase again, but it wasn't in his head—it was Hayes.

"Here we go," Hayes said. He hid the shotgun behind the front seat and opened his door. "You coming, straight shooter? Or do I have to beg you to have a good time with me?"

»»»»»

Outlaw country on the jukebox and that overloaded smell you get in a strip club: dirty sex and wrinkled currency and cheap beer all mixed like a cocktail. Through the darkness—interrupted at times by flashing neon lights above the stage—Sam couldn't tell whether the stripper was someone he'd seen around town. He thought it unlikely, but it wouldn't surprise him. He was annoyed at the woman for hanging onto Hayes. Couldn't she tell they wanted to drink their beers in peace? Sam kept his head straight and his eyes averted, tried not to stare at all the ladies wandering around Irma's, as if it was some sin to look. Meanwhile, a singer named Waylon got his education paid for by the state.

Through the music, Sam heard Hayes ask the woman, "What color eyes do you have?"

She pulled her face back, studied him. "Green. Why?"

Hayes snapped his fingers and punched Sam in the arm. "I knew it. Damn, I was right on the money."

Sam shifted with annoyance and stared into the beer bottle in his hands.

"You can't climb in there, buddy. You're too big, and it's too small."

"I know that," Sam said.

The woman took Hayes's chin between thin fingers and swung his face toward her. "You're supposed to pay attention to me, Mr. Hard-to-get."

He grew serious. "I'm not supposed to do anything. Not unless I want to."

Sam stiffened—it was that same voice he'd heard when Hayes pointed the shotgun at him. It was a hard, rattling voice, a voice that reminded him of Ryder Simms. Hayes wasn't Ryder. Sam took some solace in that, but he sounded like him—that was for damn sure.

The stripper said, "Sorry, I didn't realize."

"Tell me something. You ever see a guy in here who calls himself Jazz? He's a Marine. A little, tiny Marine, but he's got the uniform to prove it."

The woman moaned. "You're talking about Harper."

"Harper?"

"Yes, Harper. That's his real name. I call him Mr. Boring. He comes here on weekdays after work. Says the same stuff all the time. Lame pickup lines." Her green eyes, too dark for Sam to see, rolled in their sockets. She shifted off Hayes and moved to the stool beside him.

Hayes said, "What do you mean, boring?"

"Same dance. Same tip. Same lame pickup lines. Boring is what I mean. Fucking boring." She nodded at the bartender and he poured her a glass of water. "Do you want a dance? Or am I just bothering you?"

Her candor surprised Sam. Before Hayes could respond, he said, "You're bothering the hell out of me. I just want a beer. That's all."

Hayes glared at him.

"I'll leave you two alone." The woman stood, swung her hips while she walked toward a group of men in a far booth. She took her water glass with her.

Hayes smacked Sam's elbow. "See that, the son of a gun comes in here on weekdays. Now I know where to find him."

"And what are you going to do? Shoot him in cold blood while he pisses in a urinal? Rub him out while he's getting a lap dance? I don't understand the point of this."

"Oh, Sam. I wouldn't want to leave a mess for the bartender to clean up. You don't think I learned to do it better than that?"

With thin lips centered beneath dark eyes, Hayes stared at Sam. The bruise on Hayes's head looked purple in the darkness. Those eyes made Sam feel shame and fatigue, a malaise coursing through him. He reached up and touched the scar on his chin— that scar put the shame into him. That was the beginning. His eyes dropped to his scarred hand wrapped around the beer bottle.

And there was that. A wave of fatigue hit Sam—this showed on his face, in the way he moved, in the sad frustration of his thoughts. There are circles a man can think himself into, and Sam knew what this was like, how it fed on every breath. He'd thought his little son would bring him back, that the boy would frighten him back to life, but it hadn't happened. Maybe, it never would.

Sam swallowed the strip club's smoky air and said, "I wonder if you're going to tell me what it is I should be asking you. If you're going to tell me, I don't know, who I should be, now that you're back."

"Who you should be now that I'm back? Jesus, pal." Hayes turned from Sam to his beer. "I'm sitting with a guy, he has everything he could want, and he's like a damp towel crushed into a dark corner."

"You got sandbags piled around your damn property. It's set up like you expect to be overrun any second." Sam sensed Hayes shift beside him.

"I know it looks weird. Hell, it is weird. Call it force of habit."

"Force of habit? I want to know what other habits you've formed."

"I'm going to make it a habit to be here on weekdays."

"And you're going to put the guy in the dirt, right?"

"That's right."

"But why? You still haven't told me why."

"Last time," Hayes said, "when you dropped me off, you wanted to know what it was like over there."

"No, that's not how it—"

"You wanted to know. Whether you admit it or not, you wanted to know."

Sam shrugged and closed his eyes. Slowly, he opened them again and looked at Hayes.

"You can't imagine how they treat a dog over there. And it's not, like, something they do on purpose. I mean, who you going to feed? You going to feed your son and daughter, or you going to feed a dog? I just can't get it out of my head, though, man. These skinny fuckers, mangy kinds of dogs. And they got flies all around their heads and in their eyes and, man, it just gets to me. We had to shoot them. You'd think that's the worst of it, the killing of the dogs. It's not, though. Hell, Sam, that's the good part because you know—you know it right fucking here—that-that son of a gun is thankful to get shot. I shot so many dogs... I lost count, to tell you the truth. And this thing about Jazz, I'll tell you what it is—I'll be honest with you. When I went to see him, he asked me about you. That's right, pal. I'm in his office to sign up for the Marine Corps, and he's asking me about you. He says he went up to your mom's place, left his card on the door. I ask him how he got past your dogs..." Hayes stopped speaking. His eyes touched on something from the distant past.

"I never knew," Sam said. Again, his fingers went to the purple scar on his chin, traced it like embroidery.

"He says to me... I'll never forget it. He says to me, 'You ever hear about war dogs, Hayes?' And I told him that he should leave you alone. That it was me he wanted, you know. I said, 'I'm the one you want because Sam's got a whole life to live out here. He's got a chance with everything.' And it was like he stared right through me and just tied me to him—I can't tell you how it was, except, I just said he wanted *me* and to leave you alone."

Hayes looked at him, his eyes damp and bright in the smoky air. There it came again, the sharp edge of shame in his throat. It burned a place behind his eyes. He clenched his teeth, scraped the beer bottle against the bar.

"I didn't mean to get in the way. I just didn't want anything to happen to you. So, that's what I said, what I did."

Sam stood and grunted as he adjusted his coat. "You know where the guy's going to be now. So, I need to get home for the day. I need to get home to my family. You want to put Jazz in the dirt—it's not on me. I'll meet you outside. You got these drinks?"

"Yeah," Hayes said. "I'll get the drinks."

"Okay."

"Okay."

Sam walked to the door. He hesitated while the shame still burned in his throat. *Stop it*, he told himself. *There's nothing you can do about that. What? Are you going to join up now? You going to change the past? This is who you are, and you got made into something you don't understand. So what? It happens every day.* Sam pushed through the door and cold air bit his face.

The purple scar throbbed along his chin.

<h1 style="text-align:center">12</h1>

At eighty miles per hour on the highway, the hum from the Dodge's tires filled Sam's ears, pressed into his head like a thought he couldn't control. And there were thoughts he couldn't control—they involved Ryder Simms.

Red blood.

White snow.

He pushed the thoughts away, checked the rearview mirror: The two-lane blacktop was near empty. There were no headlights behind them in the winter's fragile gray—this was Sunday in a small town. A few sets approached from the east, dim yellow points in the distance. "I'm surprised you let me drive," Sam said. "I missed this car. Right now it's just you and me. It's our road."

In the passenger seat, Hayes shifted and tapped at his window with one knuckle. "I figured I could let you do some work—you got it inside you."

That "it" again, whatever it was. Sam smirked. He remembered Hayes saying a similar thing to him once. Like usual, they were getting into trouble, two teenagers up to nothing good. They'd driven out to an assortment of abandoned homes and trailers, twelve miles or so from town. Hayes thought they might salvage some metal, or find anything at all worth selling. They stopped the Dodge in front of the best-looking place—it wasn't charred to embers or leaning at an odd angle—and stared at it from the property's edge.

Through the chain-link fence, Sam studied the windows in the house. They were black as the night and the place did, like Hayes said, appear empty. Warm air pressed at Sam's glistening neck, sucked sweat from his pores. His T-shirt was wet under his arms and on the flat of his belly. He gripped the chain-link fence with two fingers and rattled it. No dogs rushed out to snarl at them—again, like Hayes said, they could cross the yard without being noticed. Sam stepped back and surveyed the trash-littered yard beneath the half-lit moon. He said, "You sure nobody's home, Hayes? I swear to God, if there's—"

"Nobody's home, Sam. I promise you. I mean, look at this place." Hayes gripped the fence, shoved his right boot into it, and scaled the steel mesh. It rattled with his weight. "You can either wimp out on me, or you can help a guy out. What's it going to be?" Hayes reached the fence's summit, threw a leg over the top, and dropped down onto the other side. He glared at Sam through the fence and said, "Do you have any balls? Or are you a little girl?" With his cheeks pressed up near his head and his mouth turned sour, Hayes added, "Are you ever going to have it, or what?"

There it was—the "it." Sam shook his head. He glanced at the house again—windows still black as mud—and started to climb. When he dropped onto the other side, needles of pain biting into his knees, he said, "Well, what now?"

Crouched and silent, Hayes moved through the yard. When they reached the house, he put his hand to a window and peered through its thick blackness. "I don't see shit, man. We're good to go. Take a look if you don't believe me."

Sam's throat clenched, and he felt his stomach tug at his chest. He didn't want to be here, breaking into a house with Hayes, but he also felt aligned with his best friend, as if they were welded together. He placed his hand on the window and squinted through the glass—he saw nothing but vague furniture shapes. When he turned around, Hayes had a large rock in his hands. "What are you going to do?"

"Watch out."

"What the fuck?"

"Out of the way, buddy. We need to get in there." Hayes hoisted the rock and rocketed it through the window with both hands. The window shattered. From inside the house, the musty smell of mold and age hit them. "See, the place is abandoned. Just like I said."

"I don't know. Something doesn't smell right in there."

Hayes said, "It's just because nobody cleaned it up, took out the garbage and old furniture." He lifted himself over the windowsill and vanished into the house's darkness. His voice floated out to Sam: "Let's go, buddy. Are you in, or are you out?"

Seconds later, Sam, too, was inside the house.

"What are we looking for?" Sam squeezed out the words, spoke through tightened lips.

Hayes didn't bother to whisper. He moved past an old, rotted couch and a television smashed into pieces. "I just wanted to see it, that's all. Maybe there's something we can take to the salvage yard."

Along the bottom of a far wall, below a framed image of a face he couldn't make out, Sam noticed the drywall torn away and stacked in a waist-high pile. "Looks like somebody else got to the pipes and wires."

Hayes moved into a kitchen area with tile flooring. Sam followed. The house was heavy with darkness, and the smell—a wet stench that reminded him of day-old vomit and the bottom of trash dumpsters—was stronger. It tickled his nose. He tried to control the muscles in his throat as they contracted and released. In the kitchen, the sink and fixtures were gone. An empty hole remained where the refrigerator once stood. Hayes put his hands on his hips, shook his head. Sam opened some of the cabinets. All were bare except for one near the sink. It held two cans of black beans and a package of linguine pasta. He lifted the pasta package and waved it at Hayes. "You got dinner if you want it."

Hayes said, "God, what is that smell?"

"I told you." Sam tossed the package onto the counter. "It's no good, man."

Hayes moved through the kitchen and entered a long hallway. Again, Sam followed. He watched as Hayes peeked into the first room. "Anything there?"

Hayes shook his head and moved to the next room. He moved

past that and toward the third room.

Sam's throat clenched and released. He tasted the smell now as if it were soup lingering at the back of his mouth. It was wet garbage and old milk and food gone to rot. Sam caught up to Hayes and stood behind him.

Hayes opened the third door.

The smell that exploded from the room caked the inside of Sam's nose and, to a large degree, the inside of his mind. It was the putrid odor of a thousand marshes bottled and concentrated, the stench of dead animals collapsed into one burning cloud. Sam's eyes, without his trying, clenched tight—he forced himself to open them. Hayes moved into the room and stared at the two lumps in the center of the piss-stained carpet. Sam stood just inside the door. With one hand, he pinched his nose. "Oh my god. What the hell happened?"

Hayes stared down at the bodies as if frozen.

Sam stared, too.

There were two dead dogs huddled together on the carpet, two medium-sized dogs with floppy ears and long snouts. Their bodies were almost melted into the floor, carcasses unraveled like dough too soft to roll. The twin prisons of their rib cages poked through loose skin and piles of short fur. Sam said, "They look like hounds, or a breed like hounds."

"Now, they're nothing. They're not dogs, hounds, or anything else."

"Who would do this?"

Hayes arched his gaze toward a corner of the room. Sam followed it and saw two large bowls, both empty. It occurred to him then: Somebody had left the dogs there, maybe planned to return. They'd run out of food and water. These two dogs died of hunger and thirst. And it was incredible, Sam thought, that they didn't eat each other.

That's what humans would have done. He was certain of that.

Sam turned his eyes back to the fleshy mounds melted into the carpet.

As if called to attention, Hayes rotated on his heels. He pointed a twitching finger at Sam and said, "You and me have a couple graves to dig. We can't leave them here like this. It's not right and I won't let it happen."

Sam noticed he was still pinching his nose. He released his hold, let his hand drop to his side. The smell ran up through his nostrils and into his brain. He squeezed his lips together and tried to hold back the moisture forming in his eyes. "I'm with you," he said. "Let's put these two in the ground."

Hayes tapped the Dodge's window with a knuckle once more, brought Sam back into the present moment. "Up there"—Hayes said, lifting a finger and pointing toward the sky with lazy precision—"that's the high ground. Good position, you know? If we ever need it."

"I guess that's true." Sam cleared his throat and checked the speedometer. He felt like pressing the Dodge to its limits, wanted to find the outer edge of machine possibility. Perhaps, he wanted to see Hayes transform from the plain-faced man he'd been since he told Sam about his plan to kill Jazz. "You're right. High ground is the best ground."

"I'm fucking with you, Sam." Hayes shrugged and tapped the window again. "Just fucking with you, that's all."

"Yeah—I know that."

"We had these night vision goggles, you know? Same as when you play a video game. I swear, I could watch a native take a dump on an ant hill with those fuckers—it could be pure dark. No stars. No nothing. I could see it all, man."

Sam didn't know how to respond. He gripped the steering wheel, checked his mirrors. A set of daytime headlights appeared a quarter mile or so behind them, began to gain ground. He tried a glance at Hayes. Found the guy staring at the highway, that same plain look on his face.

After a moment, Hayes said, "Erin get sick at all? You know, with the baby and everything?"

Sam shook his head. "It was pretty easy, I guess. No morning sickness. Nothing she complained about anyhow. And the kid, he was pretty quiet. Still is." A pang of homesickness punched at Sam's heart. "She pulls out her boob, and that's all there is. From my end, anyway."

"Shit, man. It's easy for you. You already did your part."

"Yeah," Sam said, and half smiled. "You're right."

"Man, on my flight home from Houston—I swear to god—this girl sat next to me. Short shorts, okay? And she had those kind of tan legs you see in magazines." Hayes hummed and slapped his chest with a hand. "This girl stopped my heart. I almost proposed after they gave me my peanuts. Right there on the flight, just, 'Miss, will you marry me?' I didn't do it, though. Wanted to."

"Why not? You talk to her?"

"No. Hell no." Hayes drew out the hell, made it last a long time. "You think a firefight will make you piss your pants? Try talking to this girl. I developed a stutter right there. 'May—may—may I ha-ha-have some pea, some pea, some peanuts, miss?' Oh my god, this girl was beautiful."

Sam laughed, felt the familiar connection pass between them in the car, the two of them chuckling and spinning forward at eighty miles per hour, the Dodge rumbling in affirmation.

Hayes smiled and adjusted his seat belt. He leaned back into the seat and closed his eyes. "Man, I'm tired, Sam. So tired from everything. I just want to sleep. I feel like I could sleep for weeks, months."

"You want me to take you back home?"

Hayes didn't answer.

Sam cleared his throat and said, "This can wait, Hayes. Or, we can grab a case of beers and take them back with us—hang out like high school."

With his eyes closed, Hayes said, "I want music and booze. It's the only language I speak right this second. It's all that wakes me up."

"So, I'm not taking you home?"

"Why do you care?"

Sam paused, thought how to answer. He told himself: *Act like you don't give a damn, that's what you do.* "Just making conversation, brother. That's all it is." Sam turned his gaze back to the mirror, saw the pair of headlights still approaching in rapid advance. "God," he said, "this fucker is cooking."

A second later, red and blue lights flashed—a highway patrol car.

Sam said, "I think I'm going to get a ticket."

Hayes ignored him. He wasn't asleep, but he looked like a man in the depths of a dream.

The highway patrol officer approached and said, "Eighty miles per hour on the highway." It was not a question, but a pure declaration—an indictment. He rested one hand on the gun at his hip, hooked the opposite thumb in his belt, and grunted. "I always get one. Every single day. Some young guy out to break a speed record. You do know what the speed limit is here, huh?"

Sam said, "I do, sir."

"Good. You know you broke the law. Have you been drinking today?" The officer leaned into the window, raised an eyebrow at Hayes in the passenger seat. "Your buddy looks conked out. Maybe he had a few?"

"I had one beer. That's it. My buddy was in the service, a Marine," Sam said. "He's back home. It's like a little celebration, I guess."

"Look here. Follow my finger without moving your head." The officer swung his hand through the air, watched as Sam's eyes followed his raised index finger. "So, you're just a lead foot is all. Let's see your license and registration. Proof of insurance, too." The officer straightened and only his midsection—gun, baton, taser, brown shirt stretched tight against bulging belly—was visible in Sam's window.

Sam leaned across the car for the glove compartment, but Hayes lifted a hand, pressed it into Sam's chest, and shoved him back into the driver's seat. A grunt came from Sam's throat, drew the officer's attention.

The man leaned down into the window. He centered his slow-moving eyes on Hayes, squeezed both eyebrows together and let a phrase drip from his mouth. "You got a problem over there?"

Hayes, eyes closed and hands resting lifeless on his thighs, said, "Too many problems to count, but none you'd understand." With a slight smirk on his face, Hayes added, "Mister Officer, sir."

Sam, motionless, let the next few moments unravel as if he were a mannequin in a store window. There was a fear inside him that would not let him intervene, some dark shadow that fell across his heart, made his throat close and his lips press tight together.

"You want to be a smart-ass, I guess I can make your life difficult."

Hayes shrugged. His eyes remained closed, his face slack and pale. "Isn't that what this is, you making my life difficult? But anyway, there's not a damn thing you can do to make my life difficult. I got a few things happened to me that a guy like you couldn't even dream up. It's a real hoot, you know?"

"The kind of guy I am—I'll tell you, I'm a law enforcement officer."

"Where I've been, laws are a joke not worth telling."

The officer shook his head. "And where the hell is that?"

"Forget it."

"No, we're past that. You might be a vet, son, but it's my job to enforce the laws on the highway. I need you to step out of the vehicle—do it now." The officer rested one hand on the Dodge's door, eyeballed Sam and said, "You, too, driver. Get on out."

"No," Hayes said. "I don't think I will."

"You don't think you will? I'm going to tell you once more. I need—"

"You don't tell me shit." Hayes grinned, a slow, wide smile that seemed a beacon in the flat landscape of his face.

Sam unbuckled his seat belt.

The officer took two steps back from the Dodge, drew his gun and leveled it in the general direction of Hayes. "You're going to get out of that car, and you're going to do it right now."

Behind the officer, a trio of cars passed on the highway. The metallic grins of bumpers shot forward, pointed toward town. Sam thought he saw a small boy peering at them from behind a sedan's rear window. He wondered: *The hell do people think of us right now?* There was no denying that a highway patrol officer's gun was pointed at him, that his friend Hayes was a little fucked in the head, that Erin might need to get some bail bond money together. *This situation,* Sam thought, *is a first for me, a worst for me.*

"Get out of the vehicle and keep your hands in the air. Do it now."

Sam slowly unlatched the driver's side door, dropped one booted foot into the dirt, then the other, and climbed out into the night. He held his hands near his head. "He's just a little messed up, sir—that's all it is."

The officer nodded to one side and said, "Move to the rear. Keep your hands in the air, like I said." He pivoted to his left, moved toward the Dodge. "Now, you going to come out of there? Or do we have to make this more than it is? I don't want to hurt you, son."

From inside the Dodge, Hayes said, "Hurt me? That's funny."

"Get out—this is the last time I'm going to ask."

"Hurt me?" Hayes repeated. "Hurt me?"

Sam, at the Dodge's trunk, his hands still near his head, peered through the rear windshield and saw Hayes lift his face toward the sky. Loud as a raven's cry, spiritless as a dial tone, Hayes began to laugh.

13

You need to know the way it is, that from inside this place he'd lived all his life—as wide open as it was—everything in the outside world seemed like a fog, like a mirage that shimmered and faded as Sam stretched himself toward it. How Sam's mind worked—that's the way most of the men he knew grappled with their lives. That is, if they grappled with anything. See, they lived in the desert, a place that burned hopes and dreams like it burned smooth skin. You could live in nature in the desert beauty. You could live alone in the desert solitude. You could scream at the top of your lungs in the desert silence. But none of that made you part of this big old world, the world beyond the sparse landscape. None of that put you on the real map. Always, Sam found himself removed, set against the natural flow of things and people and humor and music and love and thought. For Sam, that meant everything he did circled back to his origins. It meant that he'd always be what his daddy was, a working stiff and a journeyman, a drifter of one single place. You are where you live, Sam knew. You are your family.

There is no fighting that, never was.

Yes, he feared his tiny son back at the apartment, but he also mourned for him. All the kid had was Sam, and Sam knew that wasn't enough.

It wasn't close to enough.

It was true these thoughts and fears might all be a symptom of Sam's age, that his malaise, his conditioning, sprang from a fear of self that was common to a boy turning into a man. But to know what you are, and to know that you are perhaps meaningless, is a harrowing revelation, an epiphany that dissolves the thin membrane between action and thought. Sam questioned everything, but he did so in a way that pointed toward meaningless answers.

When he first started to think about killing Ryder Simms, it never struck Sam that he would act—it was a fantasy at best, an imagining. And because he didn't think murder a possibility for him, it never struck Sam that things could go wrong. Yet, things had already gone wrong for Sam. It was a horrible wrong that he'd been born and sentenced to a life directed at death, a life directed at final rest.

Oh, hell.

Judge me, Sam thought to himself, *if you think it'll help.*

Before Today

One Sunday morning, a few weeks after he burned his right hand to pieces, when he could grip a steering wheel, Sam Carl left his wife and young son in their shoddy apartment, started up his Chevy, and rolled onto the highway. He left early, before seven, because he knew Erin and Reagan would sleep until nine, the two of them huddled together in the bed like kittens. Not that Sam didn't enjoy being at home with Erin, but he'd felt his throat tighten the previous few days when he knew they'd watch kids' movies and play Scrabble through the afternoon while Reagan bounced on the couch. Small-town malaise, Sam figured. It had little to do with his family. But for whole days, he found it hard to breathe—Sam knew this might have more to do with what had happened to his hand and not hearing from Hayes, who was still far, far away.

He was afraid. For himself. For Hayes. For the life that kept unraveling before him. It was a life that didn't move, and yet kept moving. A life that stayed where it was and kept on being what it was while he got older, and became no different. He was still the same Sam, but a lesser Sam because the time to be another Sam—to him—had passed, left him standing on a vacant corner.

The Chevy stuttered through a lone stoplight. It was a stark desert winter, and a light dusting of flat white snow outlined the hills at a quarter mile's distance. He throttled eastward and passed John's Place, the trailer park, and an assortment of antique stores and thrift shops. At the town's edge, where a liquor store gleamed in the pale dawn next to the county fire station, Sam turned north. The highway gained elevation and ribboned through low hills dappled with imprecise boulders. He was in the snow after half a mile, and the landscape took on soft-edged characteristics—the cacti and small bushes were white mounds beneath angular Joshua trees.

Sam thought: *Sometimes I feel like I am somewhere I don't recognize.*

The highway reached a plateau. Sam pressed the throttle, and the Chevy shot forward, hummed toward a distant smattering of homes visible against a flattened landscape of snow. Another odd thought shook Sam as he accelerated into the road's swooping curves. *I guess*, he thought, *I'll say hello to Ryder Simms. He won't be happy to see me, but I'd like to pay him a visit. And maybe*, Sam told himself, *Ryder has some news about Hayes.*

Out here, where the dirt road stretched like a misshapen finger toward the cabin where his friend Hayes was raised, the snow was piled a foot high. Sam gunned the engine to plow through the deep snow. The Chevy's front tires spun once or twice, but he piloted the truck within sight of the cabin. He killed the engine and climbed out to stand in the snow with his breath visible. It came in tiny puffs and drifted toward the sky before vanishing. "I wonder if the fucker is even here."

The words died in Sam's ears—there was nobody around to hear him.

He huffed in cold air and turned in a circle. The odd thing about this swath of land was that it dipped below the horizon. Other homes, though within a few acres' distance, were not visible. In turn, the cabin, too, was hidden from view.

Sam found this fact both fitting and disconcerting.

His mind flashed to the day he'd faced Ryder Simms inside the cabin. His heart pumped like a piston and blood ran to his temples. The memory warmed his body faster than he expected, even with the snow around his boots and the cold air swirling. That was the day Sam had felt his own confidence burst and run out of him like water from a cracked glass jar. No, it wasn't confidence—it was his manhood. It was the piece of him that Sam knew should always fight, the piece of him that should take pleasure in violence. Because that was what a man was: a violent animal with hatred running like gasoline from his toes to his head.

A real man, like Hayes, was a soldier and a killer.

And maybe Ryder wasn't quite that, but he'd knocked Sam out and left a scar on his chin, a reminder that he'd been knocked down and put into blackness by another man.

Sam looked down at his bandaged right hand. Often, the hand felt numb, but now it ached like a bad tooth. Sam didn't quite understand how this could be, but somehow the bandaged hand loosed a series of ill-gotten memories. Yes, there were his thoughts about Hayes in the war. But more cutting was the memory of Ryder's swooping hand, the butt of the Luger pistol plowing into Sam's chin. And the first time he'd kissed Erin, his wife—how, he wondered, could the deformed hand reveal this thought? He recalled the look on her face, how she'd let her eyes dart to Hayes after kissing him. His stomach dropped when he thought about it, when he let the vision hover too long. He begged himself: *Stop thinking these tired, futile, fruitless thoughts.*

And there was another burning impression that his mangled hand signaled—to him and to others. That he could do violence to himself. And, if he could do that, why couldn't he do it to others? Sam thought, yes, he sure could do it. And maybe, if the world put him in the right place, he would.

He gritted his teeth and stared at the cabin for a long moment. He wondered what the hard, old man would do if Sam showed up at the front door. Sam's mind flashed to the Luger—it was still there, beneath the Chevy's front seat, a parting gift from Hayes before he went to war. What had he said? *"Keep hold of it for me,*

Sam. You got it back, and now I'm asking you to keep it." After Hayes was gone, out to sea, to war, to death, Sam had hidden the Luger beneath the Chevy's front seat—a vague notion in his head that he needed protection. From what, he could never name. Fitting, Sam thought, to knock on Ryder's door with the Luger in his coat. More than fitting—it was proper.

Sam reached beneath the Chevy's front seat and, after probing in the dark, wrapped his fingers around cold steel. And when, a few seconds later, Sam stood in the cold snow with the blue sky gazing down on his whole world, he happened to have a loaded Luger dangling from his left hand like a perverse pendant. The gun tapped lightly against his thigh and, beneath the angular edge of his chin, the thin scar throbbed. Sam did not think then about his firstborn son, nor did he think about the mother of his child.

14

"The hell are you thinking, man? We got a shotgun in this car." Sam spit out the lowered driver's side window. Cold air hovered in the Dodge, made his cheeks burn red. He stared at the apartment duplex—gray stucco walls and broken front window—where he and Erin slept, ate, and worried about their son's future. "You are so damn lucky that cop didn't take you in or search the car. I don't understand you, and I haven't understood you for a long time."

Hayes lowered his window, dangled his hand outside it. The cold did not appear to bother him. He picked at his teeth with a finger and said, "I'm just looking for a fight, Sam. What can I say?"

The lazy sounds of a desert afternoon filtered into the car: the call of black crows somewhere out of sight, sporadic engine noise from the highway a quarter mile south. From his seat, over the square-roofed duplex, Sam studied the hills through the coming darkness. Their soft peaks undulated and faded from his vision, shadows into dusk.

"You can say you won't do it again. I got a kid in that apartment, Hayes. I can't be in a county jail cell worried about bail money and citations." Sam controlled his anger. He knew it would do neither of them any good to argue—life's trajectories were beyond argument. "I mean, I get why you were upset, but let the fucker have his power trip. He's a cop. That's his job."

"I couldn't take the way he looked at me, you know? I couldn't see how—"

"You had your eyes closed, buddy."

Hayes nodded but said nothing.

"You didn't even see how he looked at you."

"I heard him. That voice. His tone, that's what. Like how you're talking to me now." He paused. "Besides, he let us go, okay? Soon as I said who I was and where I've been."

Sam counted a few measured breaths and said, "Okay, buddy. Whatever you say. I guess that's what being a war hero gets you. I'm just saying I can't get pulled into something like that. Not now, not with my kid." Sam saw Ryder's face. It appeared to him like a phantom, the old man's mouth and cheeks and forehead screwed into a pained grimace. Those black eyes, too, he saw the eyes—they were clear and inky in his memory.

You're a liar, Sam thought. *You're a goddamned liar.*

Hayes shrugged and opened the door, pulled himself upright and ambled toward the duplex. He walked to the wrong door— the duplex's other half belonged to a woman who worked the counter at a local liquor store—and tried the latch. It didn't open, and Hayes pulled his hand from the door, turned to Sam.

Sam poked his head out the window. "It's the other door."

Hayes sauntered across the building's front, stood in front of the other door, and knocked twice. The door opened and yellow light flooded onto the dirt driveway. Hayes looked like a large, hulking shadow.

Sam watched Erin wrap her arms around Hayes, pull him inside, and peek back at the sharp outline of the Dodge. He put his hand out the window and waved: *I'm okay*. She hesitated, watched him for a moment, and drifted into the building. "I better get in there," Sam said to the night, "before some kind of trouble starts up again."

Before Today

Sam trudged through the snow toward the cabin and left a dark trail of footprints along the uneven road. He shoved the Luger into the inside pocket of his coat and zipped up against the cold. The skin on his face felt windburned and icy. Damn winter was getting to him. His hand throbbed so hard, he felt it in his shoulder. As Sam rounded a long bend, the cabin came into full view. A white pickup truck sat alongside the structure, its hood dusted with snow. Sam marked the pile of garbage near the front door, evidence of a long overdue trip to the county landfill. No smoke rose from the stone chimney. Sam wondered if Ryder was inside. There were no footprints around, and that meant Ryder hadn't been outside for the last few hours. The best Sam could tell, it had stopped snowing around five or six that morning. *I'll just look in the window*, Sam thought, *see if the man is around, if he wants to talk.*

Sam moved toward the cabin. A hawk took flight from a Joshua tree near the property's edge and Sam stopped to watch as it spun toward blue sky, twirled, and sailed over his head. Sam moved forward again, listened for any movement inside the place, but the snow-blanketed desert was still, and the cabin was silent. Sam stomped his boots as he ascended the porch steps. He put his hand to the cabin's window, tried to shade it from the sun so he could see into the place. Like he remembered, a thick blanket covered the window from the inside—he could see nothing. Sam placed his ear against the window and listened. It was the same. Nothing.

Maybe he should check around back, see if there were any signs of the old man there. As Sam turned to descend the steps, he heard the cabin's front door swing open slowly. Then he heard an unmistakable click: It was the sound of a lever-action rifle, a hand flipping the lever and letting a round slide into place.

Behind Sam, Ryder Simms said, "You miss me, boy? That what brings you out here to paradise?"

»»»»»

"You go ahead and take a seat right there, boy." Ryder motioned toward the futon with the thin cushion on it. The metal back was covered by a threadbare flannel blanket. Ryder stood near the wood-burning stove with the rifle resting on one shoulder. He wore a flannel shirt and patched Levi's, black combat boots with laces trailing like whiskers.

Sam sat on the futon and looked around the dark cabin. While Ryder stared through him with cut-glass eyes, Sam unzipped his coat and let it hang open. He wanted the Luger where he could reach it. The place looked like it had a few years ago. Newspapers piled in small stacks, magazines and books strewn about the thin carpet. The wood-burning stove wasn't lit, and the place was only a few degrees warmer than outside. Sam's breath drifted out in front of him like a cloud. The kitchen area, too, was like before. All available surfaces were covered with spice bottles, canned vegetables, soup, and canned fruits. A half-eaten loaf of Wonder Bread was open on the wood cutting board near the sink. "You need a woman up here, Mr. Simms," Sam said. "You can't keep it organized, at least it doesn't seem like it."

"Oh, I'm alright. Never been one for romance." Ryder cleared his throat and tapped the rifle with a palm. "Like my boy, you know? Hayes is the same way. He's—"

"Never been one for romance."

"That's right. My boy knows. I taught him. Ain't no happily ever after in this life. Never was, and never will be. Besides, a woman can drive a real man just nuts, make him crazy as a dog. You ever seen a dog about to die?" Ryder didn't wait for an answer. "He starts barking off at shadows and voices, stumbles over his feet like a junkie. It's a sad story when a dog's mind gives up."

Erin's face surfaced in Sam's mind. He prevented a smile from crossing his face. Let the old man think what he wanted about Sam, but Sam loved Erin—he couldn't live without her, in fact. Not now. All this stuff about a dog's mind giving up—what the hell was that? "Say," he said, "you heard from Hayes at all?"

Ryder grunted and shook his head. He moved to the window, pried away the blanket with one finger, and peered outside at the snow. "He don't talk to me about nothing." The old man turned back to Sam and leaned against the wall. He cradled the rifle like it was an infant. "Hayes, he's got a thousand things he wants to hate. I'm number one on his list."

"And why's that, sir?"

"Because I hit him when he was a boy." Ryder chuckled softly and shifted his feet. "A boy don't forget that."

Sam lifted a hand to his jaw. With one finger, he felt along the raised ridge of purple scar tissue. "No, sir. I guess he wouldn't."

A laugh boomed from the old man's throat—like gravel shaken in an old tin can. "I remember I hit you, boy. I remember that." He spoke like a child, a creature pleased with himself beyond reason. "I remember it so damn good—woo-wee!" His whole body shook, and the rifle's nose tilted in his arms.

Sam said, "I never did tell you how I felt about that."

"That what you came here for? You want to tell me how you feel about me? That's the biggest bit of sissy-talk I ever heard. Tell you what I feel. I feel like you should be in that fucking wasteland next to my boy. You should be over there killing them towel-head sons of bitches. You too good for that, or what?"

"It isn't for me."

Ryder clicked his teeth. "It ain't for you."

"That's right."

"Well, then. What is for you? You get a job curling ladies' hair?"

Don't answer, he told himself. But, like so many times in his life, Sam ignored his gut instinct. "I'm a short-order cook in town."

"Hall-lee-fucking-loo-yah! That what happened to your hand there?"

Sam nodded, took a deep swallow of dank air. "It's just for now, while I look for something that's better."

"Least you have a job, boy. Better than the average, I suppose."

"Right," Sam said. "Better than none is what I'm left with."

"More than most of us, ain't it? You pansies all think the world owes you good times and butterflies. I'll tell you what, this world's all teeth and bullets, buddy. It's nails and sacrifice. Sandpaper. Ask my son—he's over there, someplace I never been, a place you won't go, and he's got sons of guns trying to plug his ass with lead." Ryder sniffed hard, spit a gob of saliva onto the threadbare carpet. "I learned a few things in my time. Pain's one. And giving pain's the other. One of those hurts less. Let's see you can tell which one."

"An old man's riddles... shadows and lies." Sam clenched his teeth in anger. To see this old bastard use Hayes as a symbol of pride in his own life seemed perverse, decrepit, twisted like the mind of a killer.

"I tell it like it is. Shadows are lies. Ain't no shadows here. Flesh and blood and sandpaper. That's all for now."

Sam chuckled and cleared his throat. "You know what you do to a kid when you hit him, how it makes him think and feel?"

"There you go about feelings again."

"Look at this place—it's disgusting."

Ryder's eyes lit, burned like shrunken candles. "So, you come up here to accuse me, huh?"

Sam's shoulders bobbed beneath his ears. He was cold. "I came up here to tell you what I think. You're one sorry piece of shit. I hope your boy comes back, but I swear he won't ever see you again."

"And how you gonna make sure of that, sissy?"

Sam reached into his coat and removed the Luger. He rested it on his knee, blinked purposefully at the hard, old man leaning against the wall.

Ryder laughed. "You don't have it in you, boy. Even I can see that."

15

Erin set a third full beer can in front of Hayes, let her eyes slip toward Sam, who downed his own beer. They sat hunched over the small dining table, him and Hayes near to buzzed but not quite there yet. Erin poured herself a glass of tap water and sat at the table.

Hayes drank some beer and said, "It's nice to be home, I suppose."

"You suppose?" Erin said. "What's that mean?" She smiled at Hayes, tried to catch the dark eyes he kept on the table's textured surface.

"It means, I'm glad to be out of my uniform. That's what it means."

"I think Hayes needs some time to adjust, Erin." Sam scowled at her. "I doubt he wants us interrogating him." *Trademark Erin,* he thought, *always asking questions until she drove a man halfway to insanity.*

Erin's eyes stayed hard on Hayes. "Aren't you going to ask about the baby? He's asleep right now, otherwise I'd bring him out so you could hold him."

Hayes lifted his chin, centered a stare across the apartment at the bedroom where Reagan slept in his crib. He'd been sleeping since Hayes arrived, an unprecedented lucky streak for his parents. Hayes said, "I always thought Sam would shoot blanks, but he proved me wrong this time."

Erin said, "That's what the local bar is for."

"Stop it. Before I get pissed." Sam shook his head at her, drank from his beer. He watched Hayes from the corner of one eye. He always felt—no, he always knew—that Erin liked Hayes, maybe loved him. And it wasn't the same version of love he had with Erin... Of course it was different. But it was still there, and it sat between them on the table like a compass needle, wheeling from one to the other as if drawn by some force greater than magnetism.

"Sam, didn't you just tell me to keep it cool? We're just kidding with you like we always do—it's back to regular in small-town America," Hayes said, and chuckled beneath his breath. "You named him after me, huh? Question is, why'd I only get the middle name?"

Sam granted himself a brief laugh and watched Erin's mouth curl to one side. He said, "We were thinking of calling the little man Pickles, since that's all Erin ate while she was pregnant. I figured that was a decent name for a boy."

"Pickles?" Hayes groaned and looked to Erin. "Is that your drug of choice now? Man, I figured a kid of yours would crave grass and cheap red wine." He lifted a hand at Sam. "Since this guy has such expensive tastes."

"It was a craving," Erin said. "I couldn't help it."

"Pickles wouldn't get him too far with the girls," Hayes offered. "I think you made the right choice. Reagan is okay. Hayes is better. But what the hell?"

"He'll be one handsome mechanic—we didn't want to screw him with a funny name." Sam knew he'd draw a laugh from Erin with that one.

It worked—her head tipped back and a melodic cackle filled the kitchen. "You are just so, so funny, Sam. I was thinking he'd be a handsome short-order cook, like his dad."

Hayes interrupted: "I don't know why you keep on with that job."

Sam coughed into his fist, pushed his beer can to the table's center. "There's nothing else in town. I do what I can." But he knew, in the deepest parts of himself, that this was a lie. Sam kept on at the diner because of habit. All of life was a habit to him, and he didn't understand how to break himself free of those chains. "Besides, it keeps our refrigerator full. Most times, at least."

Hayes leaned backward and his wooden chair groaned.

Erin's eyes shot back and forth between the two men.

"What about you, Erin?"

"I'm still trying to find something—might cost more for a babysitter than I'd make anywhere. So, here I am: the homemaker with a smile."

"Ah, you're doing good. Kids are hard, though I wouldn't know. I must have been pretty hard to deal with." Hayes studied Sam while he said it, crunched his mouth into a tight ball. "Better to follow a path than it is to die wandering. You look great, Erin. Like you did when we were in school."

Erin blushed, couldn't stop a smile from crossing her face.

A flush of rage and guilt crawled through Sam. He closed his eyes. "Erin, we should go and check on Pickles there, don't you think?"

"I'm sure he's fine." Her eyes were still on Hayes.

Sam pushed his chair back with a long creak, stood as if shot from a canon. "Let's go check on him. Both of us." He stared at her without blinking.

Hayes passed his eyes over Sam before shrugging at Erin.

"Fine, Sam—whatever you say."

He followed her into the bedroom, closed the door with an audible click. On the bed, Reagan slept. The boy breathed in a heavy, regular rhythm, one outstretched hand forming, releasing, and reforming a fist.

Erin turned with her arms crossed and said, "What's wrong with you, Sam? You think I'm not allowed to get a compliment from another man? You can't—"

"Compliment? Is that what it is?"

"What else?"

"You always liked Hayes. Ever since we were together, and before that. You used to—" He lost his thoughts as a virulent fury crossed his mind. It felt like driving through a sudden and endless storm. "I remember how you—"

Erin punched him in the center of his chest. Her knuckles were pointed and small, like bones of a bird. Sam swayed back against the closed door.

She said, "I'm sick of this man you've become. This paranoid, lost, little—"

Only one other time in Sam's life had he acted with the same fury as he did in that moment. His left hand shot out and gripped Erin's shoulder, brought her to the carpet. And Sam was on top of her, his breath hard in the skin of her throat. "I'm not little or lost or anything you say. I'm whatever—"

"Stop it, Sam." Her words hit him like bits of fractured glass, like shrapnel. "Get the fuck off of me." Her hands pressed into his cheeks, scratched behind his neck. "You better just—"

"What?" He rammed his hips against her, felt the denim barrier between them. May as well be brick and mortar. "Let you call me what you want? Treat me like a child? I didn't like how you looked at him and—"

"That's it? You force yourself on me because—" Erin grunted as she twisted her shoulders, tried to slip from beneath Sam.

He pressed his entire weight flat against her, marveled at this tiny woman who tossed first one way and then the next, a bucking bronco of a woman driving him this way and that. "Jesus, Erin. What got—"

She bit his left ear, tore into the flesh of his earlobe with drugstore-stained incisors. She shook her head like a dog yanking a rag doll from a child's hand.

"Fuck!" Sam rolled off her, came to his knees on the carpet. He lifted a hand to his ear, saw Reagan shift positions on the bed. It was then, when he saw the boy's movement, that Sam started to choke. Tears ran down his cheeks, and he heard the staccato sound of sobs. *Who is that, Sam?*

It's you, buddy. That's you sobbing in front of your wife and child. That's you, my man.

Erin stood, adjusted her top, and glared at him. "I don't know what the fuck you think you're doing, Sam."

"I'm sorry. Jesus, I can't—"

"Everything okay in there?" Hayes spoke from the kitchen

table. His voice came to them as if they were somewhere deep in a tunnel, a dark place where sound died without melody or rhythm.

Erin raised her eyebrows.

Sam got his sobs under control. Plain faced, though with wet eyes and cheeks, Sam said, "Mind your own damn business, Hayes."

Erin shook her head. She placed her fingers on her waistband. She unbuckled her pants, slid them down across her smooth white thighs. She removed her top, threw it onto the floor, stepped out of her pants. Her purple nipples hardened in the cold.

"What are you—"

"This is what you make me." She crouched, twisted onto her back and opened her legs. "Fine," she said. "This is what I'll be."

Sam tried to imagine how to defend himself, to justify what he'd done. Nothing but silence. *Silence*, he thought, *the last refuge of the doomed.* He removed his Levi's, stepped toward her, and sank to the carpet. He did not look at his sleeping son. He placed himself between Erin's legs, felt her hand glide along him, guide him into her and—when all the visions in Sam's head should have vanished, when all the rage curled inside him should have shriveled, when all his uncertainties should have drifted away like smoke—he found himself weighted down with the whole entire darkness of his life. And one single certainty did bear down on him: *It's my fault*, Sam thought. *My life is all my fault.*

I am nothing in this world, nothing but the last and final son of a forgotten father.

He rolled off his wife. In the darkness and cold, Sam lay panting, prey too tired to continue, a wounded animal waiting for its last and ultimate use.

Beside him, Erin said, "You can't even take what you're given."

Sam didn't answer.

16

Sam and Erin did not meet eyes across the table.

The futile and endless hum of the refrigerator made conversation with infrequent howls from the wind.

Hayes cleared his throat, popped the top on another can of beer. "You going to tell me the story about your hand?" He nodded at Sam's right hand.

Sam curled the hand into a fist, dropped it into his lap. He lifted his beer and finished it. "Oh, it's nothing. Just a work accident is all. I burned myself on the grill."

"Accident, huh? Lots of ways to get hurt in this world." Hayes dropped his eyes to the table and moved his lips as if tasting the inside of his mouth. "There's accidents, and there's on purpose, too. When I was overseas, I had one guy get shot in the gut. Blood, man. Just blood all over the fucking place."

"What happened?" Erin said it with a slight quiver in her voice.

"Died. A dude from Pennsylvania... played video games all the damn time." The refrigerator clicked off and the wind died. There was a long, definite silence. Hayes perked up and said, "Pickles is a good nickname. Got humor and strength—all a real man needs." He looked back at the dark doorway that led into the bedroom. "I think that's what we'll call him. Pickles it is."

"I like Pickles," Erin said.

Sam shrugged. He was tired of fighting his own thoughts. "Me too. Pickles isn't too bad. I guess he needs something, anything."

"Well, there you go. We got the nickname problem solved." Hayes snapped his fingers. He twisted his head toward Sam and said, "Now that we've decided, me and this sucker right here are going out for a good time. What do you say, Sam, you want to go shoot some pool and get drunk?"

Sam shook his head. He didn't want to stay here, in this house with his angry wife, but he wanted to leave Hayes to whatever craziness he had planned for himself. Sam didn't know how to do it, but he wanted to shake the guilt that ran through his blood as thick as venom. "I think I'm going to call it a day—I have to work Tuesday, and I think—"

"You two should go out," Erin said. She pinned him with a stare and waited for a retort. "I think you'll have a good time."

Sam bit the inside of his bottom lip. He shifted in his chair. "It's okay, Erin. We can catch up later. Like I said—"

"Why the hell am I having to convince you to have a good time with an old pal? I got something on my face? Something about me that makes you embarrassed, pal?" Hayes watched Sam with determined patience. In the apartment's shallow light, the bruise on his head deepened and his hawk nose twitched. He looked, to Sam, like a villain from a black-and-white film.

"We can't afford to—"

"I'm buying, Sam. You don't have to worry about that."

Sam looked to his wife. With her eyes, she told him to obey. And Sam wanted to tell her everything about himself. An urge rose in him to scream at her: *Hayes is crazy, Erin! He wants to kill Jazz and drag me into murder! I'm sorry for what I did to you in that room, but look at what he's dragging me into!* These phantom lines of dialogue made him feel like a character in that same black-and-white film. He felt as if he were walking around in a life that wasn't his, as if he were carrying a body that wasn't his, as if his actions—no matter what he did—were not his own. And so, like a soldier following orders, Sam said, "Yes, ma'am—whatever you say. A night on the town it is."

Hayes brought his hands together with sarcastic deliberation, a slow clap. The wooden chair creaked as he stood. "Now you got it, Sam. Now you're getting the hang of things. How's it feel to grow a pair of nice, big balls?"

What exactly "it" was, Sam still couldn't name. Balls, maybe. Or purpose. Or a willingness to squeeze a trigger and watch an old man bleed. Hayes had it, there was no doubt about that because

Hayes had—like a real man—pointed guns at people and blown up stuff and walked a tightrope between life and death. That was how the television and the radio told it anyway. *It*, Sam thought, *this fucking "it."*

Before Today

Sam glared at Ryder, a thought firing in his head: *Let's put you in the ground.* He told the old man, "I guess it's true what they say, you get old and it's a hell of a lot harder to see."

Ryder's lips pinched down at the corners. His eyes, though, brightened with his own thought. "I see the pansy sitting across from me. I can see that. Look at him, sitting there and daydreaming like the pansy he is, the pansy he'll always be. How's it feel to be sitting here on my couch while my boy's overseas? That make you feel like the pansy you are?"

Sam did not answer Ryder. He thought instead of his closest friend, the kid he remembered, the one with the hawk nose and rock-solid chin, the one who challenged a Marine in a diner parking lot, the one who signed on the dotted line because he thought it was the only thing he could do to escape this wretched man. He thought of Hayes kicking at dust and squinting at distant gunfire. He imagined his friend booting in doors and screaming at old men, yelling at the madness of the world. And this, the heart of it, grew from Ryder Simms. It was Ryder who drove Hayes to war. It was Ryder who sat here in this cabin and reaped the last benefits of liberty bought and died for. It all came back to Ryder, and he was too stupid even to know it. It was Ryder who gave Sam the scar. The son of a gun had been scarring the whole world. Hayes. Sam. He'd been scarring life itself.

Sam said, "What did you do with your life?"

Ryder set his jaw. His eyes dimmed, and he said, "I raised a son."

"Is that what you call this? Raising a son?"

"I call it the best I could do."

"Don't you just have the whole world on your back." Sam's hand tightened on the Luger. His saliva tasted salty, hot.

"I don't know what you mean, pansy. Stop with the flower talk. Give me cacti and snake fang. It's stuff I can understand."

Sam grunted.

Ryder said, "How a *man* talks."

Sam lifted the Luger and centered it on the old man. His hand shook, wavered. Sweat ran down his wrist.

"For that scar on your chin? That's all?"

Sam shook his head. "For everything. For all of it."

FNG is up to his eyeballs in the foxhole. He's nothing but sweat and grime.

Toss. Plunge.

The man is turning to dust.

"FNG," I say, "that's a deep fucking foxhole, my man. That's one hell of a goddamn grave. What are you trying to do, dig our asses back to America? You're going to dig yourself through hell and out the other side."

Toss. Plunge.

"You hear those machine guns, FNG? Those bullets got your name on them—my name, too. It's about to get a bit twisted out here in the desert, pal. Man, FNG, you're deep enough in that hole. My suggestion? Put the shovel down and clean your fucking rifle. Clean it good, because boot camp is about as far from here as Pluto. The distance from here to home is immeasurable. There's another spelling-test word for you.

"Let me give it to you straight: Pluto is quite a flight."

Toss. Plunge.

"It's, like, about as far from Afghanistan as heaven.

"What I'm saying is that this shit is about to get sticky.

"It's about to get twisted, as they say on the old TV. Me, I got the right amount of balls for this kind of work, FNG. I'm wondering if you've got the right amount of balls.

"I'm wondering if you've got the guts."

Toss. Plunge.

"Put that fucking shovel down," I say. "Put it down."

He won't put the fucking shovel down, and these explosions are getting closer. I can hear the machine-gun fire echoing down in the canyon—it's like marbles dropping in a skillet. This fucking FNG. He keeps digging.

Toss. Plunge.

Toss. Plunge.

He's up to his eyebrows now. The man is sinking into the earth.

He's going to bury himself over and—I have to admit—a grave might be the best place for him. And me, too. For all of us.

Every single one.

That shovel.

That goddamn shovel.

Toss.

Plunge.

The gunfire is right outside the wire. It's on top of us, shooting across the sky, orange flames of fire and heat.

"FNG," I say, "you mind if I get in there with you?"

"Just for a second," I say.

"For one damn second, let me get in that foxhole. While I think about what to do.

"Hell, I'll dig with you—we'll do it together."

PART III
Brothers-in-Arms

17

Still no snow. Or rain.

Hayes drove them down the dirt road, spun the tires when they reached pavement and left two long black streaks on the street. The Dodge zoomed toward Main Street, arrowed knife-like toward whatever future was left to Sam and Hayes. Sam braced himself in the passenger seat. Above them, beyond the hills, the day's last light slid backward into the mouth of approaching darkness. Sam ran his tongue across chapped lips and wondered what he was getting into with the war hero. His mind flitted to the shotgun behind the seat. He longed for the Luger waiting in his Chevy—too bad it was back at the cabin. Not that two guns made a better possibility than one, but Sam did not trust Hayes, not with that lethal look in his eyes, a half squint with those black orbs centered on the middle distance. The look reminded Sam of the day when Hayes had followed Jazz from the diner. And that day, Sam knew, was the seed from which sprouted the rage in Hayes. And the war had provided oxygen and light and nutrients for that rage, groomed it for its cruel and unusual purpose.

See the rebellious boy become the dangerous man.

Become the deadly man.

All boys play at soldier. The army guy roams the territory of American boyhood—it's a small-town thread woven into the thick tapestry of violence and war and self-lament. Hayes used to be a rebellious boy scratching a curse word into a school desk. He'd become a man who would—if provoked—use that same knife to carve a still-pumping heart from an enemy's chest.

Sam watched Hayes carefully as the Dodge slid down Main Street. The muscles in his cheeks worked hard against skin, and Sam could see a tension in Hayes near his shoulders and neck.

Also, his eyebrows seemed stuck together, like his face was frozen into anger. Hayes looked like his father. His posture and face and the twitchy way his lips moved while he formed thoughts. This spurred Sam to remember the pistol-whipping, the scathing burn of steel against his cheek and the ridge-backed scar that surfaced along his chin. The Luger's shape flashed behind his eyes. A feeling of power and manhood, Sam knew, had come from aiming that pistol at Ryder Simms. Prior to that day, he'd never seriously considered having the chance to do that—it was a fantasy, a rogue imagining. And he'd expected that same power to come from firing the pistol. Instead, he'd found guilt. And he'd found an innocence flowing out of him like sweat.

Dusk's subtle grays flashed through the windshield. The blurry outline of familiar shops reminded Sam of a time before this new rage flowered so vibrant in Hayes. This, too, was before his second tour in Afghanistan, his final few days in town before heading back to the war. They were in this same car, on this same stretch of road, headed toward the same bar. What Sam didn't understand: Why the hell would Hayes go back to the war? And he thought, *He must be searching for something, for anything.* What had he asked of his friend?

"Everything okay in the service, my man? You look stressed."

"I'm feeling good. Just wired a bit is all."

"You don't want to go back?"

"That's not it, Sam. No, it's—shit—that I want to go back." Hayes coughed and shook his head. "It's like you see in all the movies or whatever, man. They tell you when you sleep, eat, shit. They tell you how you sleep, eat, shit. Where to shoot. When to shoot. What to shoot. Mostly, that you can't shoot. You know? They supposedly got this bullshit worked out like a science, and soon it's all ingrained in you like a fat tattoo. I couldn't fuck something up if I tried. Too many people get screwed if I do. Sometimes we get to shoot, and once in a while, we get to blow something up. Tell you the truth, I kind of love it. I mean, I got nothing out here, so it's perfect for me." He paused and added, "I'm glad I went, and that I'm going back." Hayes turned left across oncoming lanes and the Dodge bumped into a gravel parking lot for a bar known simply as "Saloon."

"You know how long this time?"

Hayes slid the Dodge to a stop and dust lifted like fog around them. He flipped the ignition, and the engine died with a soft rattle. "I think the timing's fucked up in this thing," he said.

Sam said, "Did it start right up today?"

"I switched the dead battery with the one from my dad's truck."

"No you did not—you're kidding."

"Fucker was passed out drunk. He'll think twice next time."

"You're a little punk."

Hayes laughed and said, "What's he going to do, pistol-whip me?"

"He might... He's been known to do a thing like that."

"I've been known to duck. Not like you..."

Sam chuckled.

"Could be a year, for all I know."

"Jesus."

"It's all good. Without us, you can't have this." He lifted his chin at the bar. "That's what they tell me, anyway. Freedom, you know? Like it's some kind of thing I can hand you. Like it's a raffle ticket at the fair, but the thing is, your ticket is always getting drawn. You always win the prize."

A woman and an older man in a Pennzoil cap staggered out and lurched toward a pickup truck. As the saloon's door opened, a country tune drifted into the evening air. A driving beat with slide guitar.

"Who's that?"

Hayes dipped his ear to a shoulder and said, "Sounds like Ray Wylie Hubbard, old-school guy from Texas."

"I like it," Sam said. The bar's front door closed, and silence loomed. The couple climbed into their pickup and the man started it, put it in reverse, pulled out, and floored it in drive. The truck's tires spun gravel into the air. Sam said, "Fucker didn't turn on his headlights."

"Maybe he's got night vision," Hayes said, "just like me."

And in the cold night, close to a year later, Sam watched Hayes make that same left across oncoming lanes of nonexistent traffic and bump into the same dirt parking lot. *Here we are*, Sam thought. *Everything the same. Simple and small-town and so dull it hurts. Except for Hayes—he is a different person now. A war hero on the warpath. And me, I'm different, but I'm different in a way Hayes isn't.* It was guilt, he knew. For Ryder. For what Hayes had to go through to get back here, to a no-name town in the middle of nowhere. For what he had done to his wife. And there was another kind of guilt, a deeper kind: Sam was guilty of staying home while Hayes went to war. He was guilty of doing nothing. It was that feeling that burned through him again and again, a harsh and sweaty heat that swelled like an infection—Sam Carl was plump with guilt.

Hayes and Sam started with cold beers but soon graduated to warm bourbon in clear plastic cups. The bartender—a woman in a green tube top, snug black pants, and with eyes touched by crow's-feet—slid the drinks to Sam with a mixed-message look. On the one hand, Sam figured, she was happy to have the tips. On the other hand, she was nervous that the war hero and his buddy might cause some Sunday night trouble.

She said, "Should I keep your tab open?"

Sam, reluctant but certain, nodded. "We'll have one more, I bet. After these two. Hell, he might have a few more."

The bartender rolled her eyes.

Sam ignored her and carried the drinks to a place along the back wall where Hayes was rolling a pool cue across the scuffed green felt on a lopsided table. "I got you another bourbon," Sam said.

Hayes looked at him with a raised eyebrow. "This cue is bent like a thumb, man. Is it the truth or just the booze talking?" He prodded the cue with a finger, and it rolled lopsided across the table. "No wonder you're down three games to one, you're shooting with a horseshoe, my man."

Sam said, "You're already drunk."

Hayes lifted his cup and sipped. "Cheers to you and yours, Sam. My man, you did it. Had yourself a son. I never thought you would. I'll be honest." Hayes hitched his Levi's with one hand and pressed his drink to his chest. His words came out staggered and oddly toned. He shouted over the plodding country song bursting from the saloon's speaker system. They'd switched to the commercial stuff as more people drifted into the place, lifted pickup trucks and prom queens drenched in auto-tuned acoustic riffs. "I couldn't do it like you're doing it, Sam. Tell you that. It's hard to make a life in this place. To do it and stay honest, that's harder. The people. The desert. It's hard. I'm proud of you, Sam. That's what I want to say—I'm proud of what you're doing, my man. Jesus. You did it. Had yourself a son."

And the guilt burned through Sam again. *If only you knew the truth,* he thought, *you'd shoot me where I stand.* Sam swept his eyes around the bar. One side was nearly full, a line of rough faces reflected in the dusty mirror behind the liquor bottles. People had their elbows on the bar top, eyes deadened to everything but the few inches in front of them or the bartender moving back and forth like a phantom. The rest of the place was scattered with drunk or near-drunk patrons. At another pool table, a group of men talked motorcycles and tried trick shots. At the two round tables near the front door, middle-aged couples chewed stale pretzels and shared pitchers of cheap beer. He turned back to Hayes, watched him sip bourbon. Sam wanted to think that everywhere else was different, that it was this place alone where people needed alcohol and simple company to pass the time.

"Man, I should have done what you did. I should have left here as soon as I could, Hayes. There's a big world out there."

Hayes moved toward him with the slow precision of a man who knows he's drunk. "That was what I thought when I first joined the Corps. But it's not true. Nope. That's a lie, Sam. I'll tell you, it's pretty much the same everywhere. Less or more noise.

Less or more violence." Hayes lifted a finger, pointed it at Sam. "Less or more love and hatred, less or more uncertainty. Hell, it's a simple world all over the place." He paused and scoured the bar with sandpaper eyes. He declared: "And I'm not made for it—I'm too damn angry."

Sam stopped him, interrupted the anger before it could seep through the alcohol-tinged air. "I'm proud of what you did over there, Hayes."

"I appreciate that, Sam. It means something."

"And when your dad, when he—" Sam grunted and sipped from his cup. The bourbon stung his tongue. "You pulled me out of there that day. When your old man hit me. You got me out." He touched his jaw with the clear plastic cup in his hand, ran it along the ridge of his chin, stopped where the thin purple scar shone like a serpent. "That's when I knew you were a tough son of a gun. I thought, this is a man if I ever knew one. He got me out and looked that smelly, old fuck in the eyes. And he got the gun he wanted."

Hayes said, "You got the gun. Not me."

"It's up there in the Chevy. Under the seat."

"No kidding." Hayes nodded, tried another look at the bar. "I'm glad it's in good hands."

Sam drank again. The bourbon felt good on his lips, like maple syrup warmed in a pot. He hinged a hip against the pool table and finished his glass. "It's a weird-looking gun," he said. "You think about it, most guns are weird looking, like something a guy drew up from a dream, huh?"

"Probably was. How else you come up with the thing?"

"That's it," Hayes said. "You just dream it up."

"Like getting out of town," Sam said, and lifted his glass toward the ceiling.

Hayes smiled and turned to go for another drink.

Sam turned to follow and, when he did, the saloon's front door opened and a baby-faced guy in a puffy white coat over an untucked red shirt and expensive blue jeans entered. A sly little smile was pasted on his face. There it was again: Sam's stomach loosened, dropped to his ass like a sack of river stones.

Hayes paused, straightened, and moved toward the bar. Loud enough for Sam to hear, and with a low growl in his voice, he said, "Jazz, I've been looking for you. Let a United States Marine buy you a cold drink. Tell me how you feel about that?"

18

"I'll take a vodka and cranberry," Jazz said to the bartender.

He leaned sideways against the bar and studied Hayes with an icy gaze. "You're letting yourself go, brother—aren't you? I don't think that haircut follows regs, does it?"

Sam leaned against the bar next to Hayes, opposite Jazz. He could see a smirk rise on Jazz's face as he spoke. Sam tried to meet the Marine's eyes with his own, tried to say "Don't push this man here, Jazz." But there was a feeling inside him he recognized: It was the same ball-dropping feeling Sam got when they were kids and Hayes was stalking him through the desert, the feeling that—no matter what he did—Sam couldn't escape his friend.

Hayes rubbed a hand along the side of his head.

The stringy black hair, Sam felt, made Hayes look older than he was, made him look mean. A lump formed in Sam's throat, and in his head he saw Jazz's muscled forearm wrapped beneath Hayes's chin. He saw Hayes sink to the ground outside John's Place, saw again that look of rage on Hayes's youthful face when he regained consciousness.

Hayes did not speak, but instead stared at the mirror behind the bar. Moments before, he'd been almost sloppy drunk, but now he stood tall and straight, as if the buzz flowed out of him the minute he saw Jazz enter the bar.

"At least you haven't got a gut," Jazz said. "That's something to write home about. I see lots of guys come back and they take to the beer cooler and the couch. The woe-is-me treatment. That's what I call it."

The bartender slid Jazz's pink drink across the bar.

Hayes nodded at her and she refilled his cup with bourbon. On her face, worse than before, was that plastic look of irritation.

She moved toward other customers.

Sam kept trying to meet Jazz's eyes, but they didn't connect. *Why won't you look at me?* God, he needed to get Jazz alone. He needed to let the man know that Hayes had it out for him—he needed to tell Jazz that Hayes wanted to kill him. But what good would that do? Sam didn't want to believe that Hayes would kill Jazz, but he'd said it, hadn't he? He'd said it with a plain face. He'd said it with a shotgun in his hands. And if saying it wasn't enough, there were all the years in the war. A self-evident truth that Sam feared would always and forever be present in Hayes. Take that ball-dropping feeling he'd had and multiply it by a thousand. Churn all the carefree moments he'd had with Hayes and wrap them into a boiling, urgent hurricane. This, now, was the man Hayes meant to be. The man with the shotgun in his hands.

Sam leaned over the bar again, tried to catch Jazz's attention.

Jazz—he ignored Sam—sipped from his glass, smacked his thin lips, and hissed. "Tastes like freedom, doesn't it boys."

Hayes laughed the same maniacal laugh he'd loosed when the highway patrolman had his pistol unholstered and at the ready—*this Sunday*, Sam thought, *has swirled and swirled and swirled into oblivion.*

Jazz gave a sidelong glance at the odd laughter. He smirked again, a smug little expression with half-formed humor. "Well, the hell do you say, Marine? Any fine ass in here I need to know about? Or you gonna keep it all for yourself, like top-secret intel?"

"Shoot," Hayes said. "I've been gone. You know more than I do."

Jazz said, "I'll tell you, there is nothing like a Sunday-night cocktail to put me in a good mood. So, tell me about what you've been doing. How'd the Corps treat you? I'm guessing, by the looks of things, you got out." Jazz turned to Hayes and surveyed him like a man deciding whether to buy a car. He shook his head and turned back to his drink, let his eyes wander down the bar.

"It was exactly how you said it'd be."

"And you made yourself a war hero." Jazz cleared his throat. "Isn't that right, Sam? How's it feel to have a war hero as a buddy?"

Sam perked at his name. He ran a hand through his hair and swallowed. Was there something he could say to calm Hayes, a phrase he could utter to keep Jazz breathing? Or did it matter? "It feels like you should buy our drinks. That's how it feels."

Jazz grinned and shook his head. "I can buy a round or two, for old times' sake, I suppose. Been awhile since—"

Sam interrupted. "What are you up to tonight?"

Hayes swung a look toward Sam. His eyes lay still and sharp in his head. Before Jazz could respond, Hayes continued his answer. "It was exactly what you said it'd be." He turned to Jazz and settled his elbows on the bar. "I have to admit, you got me with the whole bury-me-draped-in-an-American-flag thing. You reeled me in like a fat, shiny trout. I took that bait, nice and slimy, like every other teenager."

"You read *Philosophy for Dummies* or something? That what this is?" Jazz scanned the bar with languid interest. Those fist-like muscles moved in his cheeks.

Sam—and this surprised him—felt a sudden urge to strike Jazz. The moment when Jazz drove him to the hospital drained away—it was almost as if it didn't happen. He thought back to their third year in high school, when he and Hayes both still rode the bus. Hayes didn't have the Dodge yet, and both boys were outcasts in a sea of teenagers. Second period, homeroom, was for catching up on homework, passing notes, and staring at girls. Every few weeks they'd have a presentation from someone in the community. The newspaper editor, the mayor, and, yes, one day it was Jazz who stomped into the classroom and stood up front like a five-star general, his uniform creased to razor edges and intensity burning off him like sweat. Sam could still see Jazz how he was back then—a bit younger and slimmer—but he had the same erect posture and self-important look on his face.

The first thing Jazz had said to the class: "I'm a United States Marine, and I am one bad dude, let me tell you." He'd crossed his arms over his chest and met the eyes of a few teenage boys, carried his gaze from one to the next like a sniper. "There's not one of you in here who could kick my ass, and that's for sure."

Sam heard a few girls laugh. They were in the first row, and he swore that Erin—her long blonde hair cascading across bare shoulders—laughed with them. A pang of jealousy swept him, covered his heart like fog. He thought: *I'd like to have that girl laugh at something I say.* From that moment, he plastered his eyes to the straight-shooting Marine talking down to them.

"I'm here," Jazz said, "because I want you to know there's a way to serve your country. In the Marine Corps you'll have the opportunity to use deadly weapons, drive high-performance vehicles, and learn the modern Marines' tools of the trade. But it's not just that—in the Marine Corps we teach you how to be the meanest and toughest and deadliest version of yourself."

Sam gave a quick thought, again, to Erin and the other girls. What did they think about what Jazz was saying? Did they even care? Or, did they just watch the guy's muscles move beneath his uniform? Jazz paced back and forth, rubbed his hands together as if conjuring truth from the classroom's musty air.

"I'll say it again. Becoming a United States Marine is the right move for you. And when you get out of the Marines—if you ever want to leave—you'll find yourself on the business end of a whole bunch of cash. You'll have to use it for *college*," Jazz emphasized this last word, "but you'll be the one who gets to spend it."

A few of the boys in the class chuckled. Sam turned to look at Hayes. His buddy bit the thumbnail on one hand and breathed slowly, like a bored kid in a trigonometry class. Sam turned back as Jazz stomped down the row of desks. He placed his fists on one and stared the kid in the face. "You want to be a man, son? You want to be a grown man when you get out of school?"

"Yes, sir."

"How you going to do it?"

A hesitation and then, "Join the Marine Corps?"

"Don't make it a question, kid. A man doesn't question—he

makes statements." Jazz stormed back to the classroom's front, hefted a stack of brochures and slapped them against his chest.

"There's some information in here and there's my card, too. You all can look through these and you can ask me anything you want. Just give me a call. Especially you, young lady." He slid a brochure onto the desk in front of Erin, and Sam took notice of how she used a thin finger to brush her blonde locks behind one ear. Jazz's face drained of purpose, and he stared at Erin for a few moments too long. A low whistle erupted from Hayes's pursed lips. Sam looked at him and shook his head. Some nearby heads turned, but the whistle came too low for Jazz to hear. He moved to the next row and began to hand out the rest of the brochures.

"Make sure," he said, "you don't let Mommy tell you it's too dangerous, okay? I know some of you in here are pansies, but that doesn't mean you have to be pansies for the rest of your lives. There's some momma's boys who became Marines, too—I know a few myself."

Sam waited for his brochure and when it was handed back to him, he opened it thoughtfully, read through the first few paragraphs like it was the greatest story he'd ever seen—most of the other kids did the same, but after Jazz stomped out the door and down the hall toward other classes, Sam noticed Hayes still biting his fingernails. "You going to look at that, or what?"

Hayes sniffed and clenched his jaw before saying, "That's just another scam they pull to get you killed, Sam. You know that, don't you?"

"I know it's free money, and it's something to do."

"There's lots of things to do. You want to run around and do what some buff bastard says all the time?"

Sam shrugged, looked back at the brochure, folded it, and shoved it deep into his backpack. A few minutes later, after the class bell rang, Hayes hustled into the hallway and vanished among a crowd of students. Sam noticed Hayes had left the brochure on his desk, untouched. On the front, beneath the image of a clean-cut white guy in a dress uniform, a sword splitting the twin halves of his face, were the words *Semper Fidelis*.

At the time, he'd wondered, *What the heck does that mean?*

And now, years later, Sam pushed that memory deep into his brain.

"Dang," Jazz said, "you know what's funny?"

"What's that?" Hayes rubbed a hand along his chin, shifted his feet, and moved away from the bar.

"You were always gonna be a Marine, man," Jazz continued. "I saw it on your face. If it wasn't me that brought you in, you would have done it yourself." Jazz swirled his drink, sipped, and bit into a shard of clear ice.

Hayes turned from the bar without answering and walked between the pool tables. Sam watched him lift a pool cue, lean it against a far wall, and begin to rack the table—he'd pulled himself away, sulked into his own cloud of rage, or so Sam assumed.

"You're pushing his buttons, Jazz. You know that, right?" Sam moved closer to Jazz, leaned toward him and—it hit him fast— smelled thick waves of expensive cologne. "This isn't the same kid you choked out way back when."

"They're always the same kids. Small-town kids who never change."

The urge came to Sam again—he wanted to make Jazz scream in pain. It was the same urge he'd experienced sitting across from Ryder in the cabin, and it came over him with the same sweeping certainty. His thoughts pointed him down a dark tunnel: *You're the one who keeps lighting this world on fire. You,* he thought, *you're the devil in a pressed uniform. And just because you have a flag behind you doesn't make it right.* The shape of the Luger imprinted itself on Sam's mind, pressed into his head like hot steel branding cattle. *I could hurt you,* he thought, *if I wanted to.*

Sam pulled himself from this burgeoning rage, turned to look for Hayes. His friend was lining up a practice shot on the pool table, concentrating on shooting straight with a crooked cue. *Now that's funny,* Sam thought. *And aren't we all doing that?* Looking back to Jazz, Sam said, "What the fuck is that smell?" He sniffed twice.

Jazz started, folded his brow and said, "What?"

"That flowery shit. You smell that?"

"No. I don't."

Sam leaned closer to Jazz, plunged his nose toward the man's stiff red shirt. "Well, holy shit," he said. "I think that's you. You have some kind of perfume on you, or what?"

Jazz stepped backward and glared at Sam, met his eyes for an instant and looked away, plastered his attention on the bartender's swinging hips. "I have cologne on, man. I don't expect a small-town fuck like you to know what that is, but anyway…" He sniffed and curled his mouth toward one side of his face.

Sam scratched his chin and said, "Oh, is that what that is? Cologne? That's French, right? French dudes wear that, I heard. That way Americans know when they're coming, or when they're on a train or whatever."

"Fuck you, Sam."

Sam put his mangled right hand on Jazz's shoulder, squeezed. "Don't get all mad, Mister Marine—I'm fucking with you is all. Like, you know, a joke."

Jazz shrugged him off, guzzled his cocktail. "Tell your pal thanks for the drink. And the shitty company." His eyes flitted beyond Sam. "Well, I take that second part back." A laugh boomed from Jazz's mouth. "Oh, man. You fucking morons. I can't believe it." Jazz turned back to the bar and shook his head.

Sam turned and watched as Hayes stumbled toward a group of bearded men in ripped denim vests. In one hand, he held the crooked pool cue like it was a giant penis. He stopped and swung it back and forth like he was spraying the crowd with urine. "Look," he shouted over the music, "I'm big as a pool cue." The men were not amused. Their faces flattened beneath the bar's smoky light.

Sam gulped his bourbon and sighed. "I didn't see that coming." He pushed himself away from the bar and looked back toward Jazz, studied the man's well-moisturized skin and too-expensive clothes. He said, "You better stay away from Hayes. I appreciate what you did for me." He lifted his hand, faced his palm outward so Jazz could see the intricate network of raised skin and scars. "And now I'm returning that favor. You have to trust me on that."

Sam gave Jazz one last glare and then turned to watch Hayes—he shook his head and, like a proud parent, smiled.

19

In the darkened desert, the Dodge's headlights shone like insect eyes and crept through the sandbags and broken fence. Sam parked the Dodge and floored the throttle to show off. The engine roared and, after a guttural thump, died. Sam climbed out and pulled a case of beer from the back seat.

Hayes followed.

"We'll have to stop drinking at some point," Sam said, and crouched into a sitting position on the porch steps. He ripped open the cardboard box and pulled two bottles out, handed one to Hayes.

Both men twisted off the caps and tossed them into the dirt.

Hayes said, "It's easier to keep going than it is to stop—seems like it's always that way. If I wasn't drunk back there, I swear to god. I wanted—"

"I don't think you want to do it. I don't think, and I'm being honest, that you can do it. It's the way you looked at him. You're brothers-in-arms, Hayes. Semper Fi, am I right?" Sam was not trying to convince Hayes. He meant only to describe the truth as he saw it. On the drive home, Sam had come to a conclusion: Hayes needed something at which he could point his rage, but he didn't want to act on that rage—he was too aware of the consequences. And that was the main difference between being at war and being at home. In one place, there were consequences, hard results for the hardest of acts. "I think you want to drink and spit and curse, but that's the most of it. Otherwise, you'd have done it then. Have another drink. It suits you." He motioned toward the box and flitted his eyes to the stars dripping across black sky above half-formed clouds.

"And here's another one telling me what the truth is, huh?" Hayes lifted the bottle to his lips and gulped. He looked demonic—his nose came to a sharp point in the moonlight and his forehead crumpled like a cheap gas-station map. His lips were inky black and moved against themselves like serpents. With his etched face turned into the moonlight, Hayes stared at Sam with splotchy black eyes, dark orbs pointing like the business end of a double-barreled shotgun. "Another big boy with a little bit of truth. Thinks he can go around and make the world sane." He was talking to himself, not to Sam. "Thinks he can make flowers bloom and kids giggle and, oh, make the war some kind of halfway event, a thing from a story he can't remember. Doesn't bother to remember. That's the thing... You don't bother."

"I'm up here, drinking with you. We've been at it the whole day."

"When you could be at home with your wife and son."

"You said it." Sam tasted more beer. He hunched deeper into his coat, tried to block the cold from touching the skin on his neck. Hayes wedged his upper lip between his teeth. He bit down hard and watched Sam sip from his beer. Sam knew his thoughts were irrational and shortsighted, but he couldn't stop the image from entering his mind: He saw himself—not Hayes—holding the pump-action Remington on Jazz while a wet stain spread on the man's crotch. He tried to ignore his imaginings. *No more of that, not tonight. Or ever.* "I can't remember what I didn't see, Hayes."

"Maybe that's it. Maybe you need to see something. A real thing you can't push out of your head—maybe that's exactly what you need."

Sam swept the desert with his vision, spotted the flat spot in the center of the property, the tamped-down dirt. But he couldn't tell Hayes about that. Secrets and lies. Shadows. Ryder had said something important to Sam: *"Give me cacti and snake fang."* And that's what this was, being here with Hayes, talking—in a roundabout way—about killing a man.

It was all cacti and snake fang. "No more flower talk," Sam said.

"What's that?" Hayes squinted at Sam. "What'd you say?" His shoulders hunched into themselves. He clenched a hand tight around the beer bottle.

Sam said, "It's nothing. I'm sorry, Hayes—what are you saying to me?"

"You make it what you want."

"You want me to go with you to do it, right? To kill Jazz? You want me to go with you to put him in the ground. That's what this is. Since I got up here, that's what this has been. I saw it, but I didn't want to believe it."

Hayes shrugged, spit words through his tense lips, "You go ahead and make it what you want."

Sam took in the sight of the stacked sandbags, the Dodge Dart parked alongside them, and his own big Chevy there in the darkness. "What happened to you, Hayes? I look at it and figure, okay, a few years in, but one day I hear your voice on the phone. And you've got no explanation, no story behind why you came back or how it happened."

"It comes out to a long boring story, Sam."

"A tall tale, or a tragedy?"

Hayes stood, stepped off the porch, and shuffled his feet in the dirt. He finished the beer and tossed the empty bottle at a rock. He missed his target, and the bottle rolled until it rested, label obscured, on its side in the dirt. "Both of those kinds, I suppose." He waited for a long time, decided to speak again: "You get some time to think, Sam, and you take it. And then, shit, it's just the thinking that does you in, makes you all kinds of wrong. I'll tell you about—"

"A girl?"

Hayes tilted his head, thinking. "There's no girl wants what I have, Sam. I leave all that to you."

Sam knew Hayes didn't like his own history, and so he didn't like girls—later, women—asking him about it. Hide the things you hate the most, Hayes had told him, and that keeps you sane. And it was advice Sam took. He hid the things he hated most about himself. That he was a killer. That he was a fraud and a liar and afraid to do the things Hayes did.

Still, he tried: "It's murder, Hayes. Not war."

"What's there to say? War is a kind of murder."

"You remember we were pals. We were brothers. You must have forgot all this life we've lived, our living out here and taking things day by day. It was you who left it. Not me."

"You can forget a lot when you're gone from a place."

"You can't take this place out of you, Hayes. It'll always be there."

"You sound like my dad," Hayes said.

Sam hesitated, rubbed his chin with a finger, and said, "At least he was right about that. You grow up here, and it never comes out of you—it's like blood, and it runs inside you like tar."

"I'm back, aren't I?"

Sam shook his head. "For what, though?" He looked up and watched a plane high overhead, a lone pin of light sliding past a dark background. There was an icy breeze, and bumps rose on his arms and neck. He finished a beer, discarded the bottle, and buried his hands in the pockets of his coat. There was a story inside Hayes, something he needed to tell. It was an infection there in his gut, a thing buried deep inside him and covered with fear, hatred, and disappointment. He couldn't live until the infection was gone, Sam knew. But was the story the infection, or was it something else? Maybe it was both, or neither. "You going to tell me about it? Or do I have to torture it out of you?"

Hayes twisted the cap from a new beer bottle, turned it in his hands like a silver coin. He thought for a moment and said: "I kept bumping my head against the window. It was the road. I was in that old pickup my dad had, the white one. And he liked to mash the throttle on these dirt roads. You get to a pile of boulders or a dry wash, and the man just floors the fucker, plows it through whatever's there. He always told me 'It's power that gets a man where he needs to go.' I still remember that. He wasn't right about a lot of things, but that—he was right about that. I remember I said, 'Slow down, Dad.' And I kept saying that, you know? He heard me, but he didn't listen, just kept crashing through dust. And he told me, 'Hold on to your balls, Hayes. That's what you need to do.' I swear, I've been holding on to my balls ever since.

"He put us on this switchback—this was east of here—and it was real rocky, scattered juniper and cholla all along the road. When I looked up, I saw the ravine and I thought of razor blades, how it looked cutting into the sky. We hit some softer sand, got through it, and then up-up-up. He kept pushing that truck, beat it to hell and back. He had all this spare change rattling in the ashtray and his beer cans rolled around on the floorboard. I remember this as if it was yesterday. Or tomorrow. Something like that. I tried to roll down my window and he said, 'You leave that, you son of a gun. You'll get dust in here.' And he always scratched his neck with his fingers. They were sticky and oil-stained, you know? And as we went up, I kept hearing the shocks on the truck, the suspension, and I was little then, but I knew the sound was wrong—it was doing something under there. Anyway, I didn't say much more. He kept saying how the road went bad over the winter. And, you know, I just hated his voice. I always did. It was like barbed wire against my teeth—that's how it felt to me.

"Tell you what, Sam, I used to see my dad like a character from one of those old stories, the ones from when we were kids. He was like a colorful character I might see in some weird book. He knew how to fix things, or make them work when he had to. That felt like a superpower when I was a kid. I always liked how he knew the songs on the radio. Those were his country songs. Johnny Cash and Waylon and Dolly Parton and all these others. He could sing, too. I thought that was odd. Still do. I think it was when I was about twelve that the switch flipped. In my head, this character from all the stories became a little like a monster. And I didn't understand him. What I'm saying is that I knew, from the way he was, that my dad wasn't normal. Something felt all wrong about him. And so, that's hard for a kid. I just kept saying to myself, 'You, too, Hayes. You're the same as your dad.' I thought that was how it worked, you know. It is how it works—I still think that lots of times."

Sam cleared his throat. He tasted the insides of his mouth and watched the cold, dark desert. Miles off, a pack of coyotes volleyed cackles. Pinprick stars burned like bright capers. "Sons have a choice. I hope mine does. Otherwise—"

"You think it," Hayes said, "but you don't believe it or even feel it. Okay, think it. Go ahead. But that don't make it true. All the things I did in school, when I got in trouble, that was because of the way I felt about my dad. Or didn't feel. Or thought I didn't. I'm not sure what to say about it, or how. It's just, it all went back to that. This man at my house living like a caged monster. And me in there with him. All wrapped into his habits and rage and twisted thoughts. I remember he liked to wander around the property with that shotgun, the Remington. He'd just put it on his shoulder and wander. He'd walk the perimeter. Pulling watch. The man who wandered with the shotgun in his hands. That was Ryder, my dad."

"You were saying about this trip into the hills." Sam wanted to get away from thoughts of Ryder—a swelling guilt crept into his throat. He rinsed it down with beer. *Into the abyss, you.*

"First, I'm out in the yard pulling weeds. The ones that come through the dirt like spikes. Next thing I know, he's got me by the back of the shirt and we're headed for the truck. 'Get in there, boy,' he says. 'It's time I taught you how to shoot. It's part of being a man,' he says, 'and now's the day.' We get on the highway, east toward the hills, and we turn off onto this dirt road. The one I was describing. I got nervous, Sam. Looking back, it's funny. To be so nervous about a gun. And that's where power comes from. Who's got the guns has the power. You learn that in war pretty damn quick. Of course, you need to see what you're shooting at, but first, have the guns. I was afraid of the power. That's exactly what it was. I hated that feeling—fear.

"I wanted to know if I was strong enough before I tried it. And I think that's natural. It's common to feel that, and to let fear get inside you. Anyway, we got up this switchback, way up to where I could see the tops of the hills and the sun beat down on us. When I got out of the truck, I could see down into the ravine. Cacti and juniper and lots of dirt. He says, 'Get over here, Hayes.' That same voice. And I go around to the back of the truck, and he's got the tailgate down. There's a long brown rifle on a grungy purple towel. Next to it, he's got that shotgun. There's the Luger. These three guns lying out there like jewels or something.

"I recognized the Luger, the shape of it. I said, 'That's like from World War II, right?' He says, 'They call it a Luger. It's a kind the Nazi bastards liked to use.' He picks up the Luger, holds it in the sun, and inspects it like a dentist. One eye closed, the whole deal. I laugh now. Imagine, seeing my dad inspecting some gun like he knows what the hell to look for. He says, 'It's a pretty little fucker, don't you think?' You're young and how the hell do you answer that? I was afraid, Sam. I reached out and touched the rifle. He says, 'Go on and pick it up, son.' Never, not once, had I heard him call me that before. It was always *boy* and *bastard*. Never *son*. Not one time that I could remember.

"So, I pick it up and it's not as heavy as I thought. I point it into the ravine and put my eye to the sight, like I saw in movies. I say that it must shoot pretty far. And he laughs, like he does. He says, 'Watch where you point it.' He drags me over to the edge of the switchback and tells me to aim down at a juniper tree. It's one of those with the thick limbs, a big neck coming out of the ground. Shoot, it's probably still out there. 'Get down on one knee,' he says. So, I'm kneeling, and I can feel the rocks and dirt through my Levi's, and I point the rifle at the tree. The best I can, okay? And I'm trying to hold the damn thing steady, but it's heavy and my arms are tired. 'Use your damn muscles,' he says. 'Lift it here and put your cheek here. Close your other eye and flip this.' I still remember how he said it. 'That's the safety,' he says, 'and you have to flip that off. Now it's ready to go and all you got to do is hold your breath steady, breathe in, and you squeeze the trigger. Go ahead and just breathe. Now hold it, and squeeze.'

"It didn't hurt when the rifle kicked back into my shoulder, but I kind of fall, and he grabs me by the shoulders. He says it again, he says, 'You missed, son. You see where the dust took up from the ground? That's where you hit.' My nose is all itchy from the dust and heat. My arms are tired, and I can smell the warm beer on his breath, but I ask, 'Should I try again?' I wanted to put the rifle down, to forget the whole thing. But there was something else inside me, too—I wanted to make my dad look at me like I was a man, you know?

"He shows me how to work the lever-action—'Now, see this? Flip that real hard all the way forward and back'—and the cartridge pops out of the gun and lands in the dirt. I'll admit something that I knew right then: I liked the way it felt. It was final, somehow. And certain. And it had the feeling of power I got from it. That's what I've been talking about.

"He says, 'Good. Good boy. Now go on and do like I told you. But line up this notch with that one and put it on the tree. Do it now.' He taps the gunsight with one of those twisted fingers. 'This here lines up with the end,' he tells me. I do it like he tells me and when I squeeze the trigger again, there's a *smack*. It's like a twig snapping in a fire. I'd closed my eyes, right? The sound and the clap and the kick from the rifle made me close my eyes. I hear him saying, 'That a boy, Hayes. You got just where I told you. You're a damn natural, you son of a gun.' I try to see where I hit the juniper, but it's too far off. He tells me, 'Now, we'll get you on the pistol. Every man who wants to be worth a damn needs to learn how to handle a pistol. It's like zipping your fly.' I'll never forget this: I watch him load the Luger and, at first, I watched those oil-stained fingers push and tuck. But I look up at his face, my dad. I swear, the look on his face: He's got these shining eyes and his cheeks are smooth. His yellow dog teeth are showing, and I know what it is—it's a look of pure, evil joy."

Sam finished the beer and tossed the bottle into the dirt. Both men savored the newfound silence, listened for signs of wildlife. Bobcats or more coyotes or owls in the underbrush. There was nothing.

Sam tilted his head to one side, squinted at Hayes, and said what he was thinking. "I swore, I thought you were going to tell me about the war. I thought you were going to talk to me about the damn war." He pulled another bottle from the cardboard box and twisted off the cap, tossed it hard at the darkness.

Hayes shifted slightly in the cold wind. He sniffed and coughed once into a bare fist. "I was talking about the war," he said. "The war is all I've been talking about, Sam. It's just that you don't hear me. You don't know how to listen." Hayes moved toward the porch, lifted a beer and opened it. He walked into the darkness where, to Sam, he became a thick shadow moving like water. With his boots, he made crescent shapes in the dirt and poured some beer into them.

Sam imagined liquid filling the shallow indentations.

Hayes said, "You have that scar on your chin, don't you? That scar came from my father."

"I do. It did."

"That's a story about war, too." Hayes scraped dirt over the liquid with a boot, watched as the wetness must have bubbled up like thick blood coming through the soil. "Scars and the people who make them—small acts of war."

Sam watched his friend stand in the darkness and cold. What could he say? He decided he didn't understand a thing about war, and he never would. How could he? How could anybody if they hadn't been through it? Maybe this was what Hayes was saying. Or maybe not. Maybe this was all crazy talk and shadows—God knew what it was. Scars, though. Sam knew all there was to know about scars and the people who made them. He lifted his right hand to where he could see it. The topography of tight scars etched into his palm shone gray, twisted lines without direction.

Maybe Sam did, after all, know a little something about war.

20

If you knew the light well enough, you'd know the slight lip of gray to the east meant impending sunrise—Sam knew it, and he noticed the thin clouds from the day before lifting high and, in many places, fading to nothing. He thought it might warm up today, though the night had been cold and still—they'd gotten no snow, as Hayes had predicted. Sam watched him as he scoured the desert beyond the cabin. He appeared to Sam now and again, a dark figure moving through creosote and yucca, his shoulders tilting with the shifts in landscape. Sam blew hot breath into his clasped fists as he watched. The morning was on them now, and that meant decisions. It meant a broken friendship or a sacred brotherhood. It meant, for Sam, blood or ignorance.

They'd spoken into the night... screamed, shouted, argued, whispered like prisoners. About what? About nothing and everything—history, answers, far-off places, and the wife and son waiting for Sam back home. Sam knew that Erin did not wait up for him. She'd reason that he'd been drunk last night, that he'd crashed with Hayes at the cabin or in the Dodge outside a dingy bar. And after their battle in the bedroom, after what he'd done— or tried to do—to his wife, Sam did not expect her to want him. He would not be missed.

There it was again: choices and consequences.

Not like war, he'd argued to Hayes.

But Hayes wouldn't have that part of it. "There are always consequences," he said. "Here"— he pointed to the center of his chest—"or there"—and then to his head, at the deep wrinkle that ripped through the center of his forehead.

"Not like this," Sam said. "Prison. Guilt. Can't you see that—"

"Death. Don't forget death."

"But why?" Sam didn't see how Jazz's death could revive Hayes.

"Because of what he did to me, dammit."

"He's done nothing to you. That day at the diner, that was you who—" And it was that memory that stopped Sam. He clamped his mouth shut and breathed hard through his nose. His heart thumped, and the night closed in on him. What Jazz did to Hayes, it was no different than what Ryder had done to Sam. And Sam saw what Hayes meant to affirm. He'd gone to war and maybe did horrible things, or heroic things, but Sam knew that—whatever he did—Hayes would equate himself with that moment in the diner parking lot. He saw himself as forever in debt to his memory of that day, and there was only one way to repay that debt, to regain the independence that made him a man. Sam understood—it took one moment of one memory, but he finally understood. Jazz stood between Hayes and true manhood. Like Ryder stood between Sam and true manhood. Hayes was not crazy. Sam was certain he was as rational as he'd ever been. Too rational, in fact.

This, in some ways, was the problem.

Hayes meant to kill Jazz, and he meant to do it today.

As Hayes came back through the desert and approached the cabin, Sam tried to convince himself to leave and return to his wife and son. He wanted to be home in a warm bed with a pot of coffee hissing steam at his childhood memories. He wanted the smooth skin of his wife against his belly. He wanted his son's cries in his ears. But as he watched Hayes walk toward him, Sam was overcome with feelings of loyalty and duty. He saw the two of them together, a couple of too-tough teenagers sliding through ghostly streets in a Dodge Dart. He saw Hayes grinning as he pushed a '69 Ford to its premature death. He thought about a word etched into a desk and the pocketknife hooked to his keychain, but mostly he thought about Hayes in a nameless place with an assault rifle in his hands. This hard-muscled kid with shotgun-barrel eyes seeing that he wasn't a man, not a real man. Not until he could get back home and kill the son of a gun who put him there. Sam did understand. For him, that was the easiest part, now that he had it. But the righteousness of it was another thing altogether. *I don't agree with this,* Sam thought, *but I can't let him go through it alone. He needs me—I am all that's left for him.* Sam's eyes flitted back to the flat center of the property, but his gaze was broken by a voice made harsh from cold and strain.

"It's time," Hayes said. "Cacti and snake fang. No more flower talk."

»»»»»

The Dodge's rear tire bumped over the curb as Hayes turned into the strip mall parking lot. This was where Jazz worked, the Marine Corps Recruitment Office. Convenient to the local high school and a popular barbershop, the office sat dead center in town, a beacon for the small-town kids with nothing to know but football and cheap beer. You'd use it as a landmark if you ever gave directions. "Left at the Marine Corps office," or, "go two blocks past the Marine Corps office." Like that—it was a center easy to hold.

In the passenger seat, Sam unbuckled his seat belt and leaned back against the seat. Hayes let off the throttle, and they slid by parked cars and dead grass—boxy buildings shrouded in the early morning's gray-blue mist. Hayes turned left, stopped at the next junction in the lot, and backed into an empty parking spot. He pointed at a gleaming red pickup and said, "That's his truck right there. Monday morning, bright and early. The sucker is hard at work trying to get poor kids signed up for a free trip to hell. He'll be out in a little bit, I bet." Hayes flipped the ignition off but left the key in so they could listen to the radio. He flipped a knob and Dolly Parton's angelic voice came through the speakers. "I like her stuff, man," he said. "She wrote so many songs. People don't know that about her these days."

"And then you get some pop singer doing them over again, making millions off a song that means so much." Sam clenched his teeth, thought himself insane to be sitting here. What in the hell were they doing?

"Right?" Hayes unbuckled his own seat belt. He draped his arm over the seat and brought the pump-action Remington into his lap. "What we'll do is, we'll just wait here and see what happens."

"You need the shotgun for this?" Sam traced the shotgun's profile with his eyes. He'd fired a shotgun once or twice, remembered the sore muscles in his arms and shoulder.

Hayes sniffed twice and looked at the gun. "I can see you're scared. I never said I needed you to do it. You want to go, just get out of the car and go." His gaze flipped back to the pickup truck.

"I'm not scared. That's the last thing on my mind." But Sam was scared. The fear ran from the pit of his stomach, through his chest, and into the throbbing place between his eyes. He tried another question: "Are you going to do it here?"

"We're just watching the man. That's all this is, Sam."

"Because it isn't the perfect crime to—"

"And what the hell do you know about it?"

Sam pressed his lips flat. He did know something about it. Oh, yes he did. He knew how to do and deal with the thing Hayes wanted to do—Sam was the one who knew about all this, every single bit of it. He said, "I guess it's good I brought the Luger. Maybe I can keep you in check." He licked his upper lip and waited. He'd grabbed the pistol from his truck before they left. A last, fleeting urge he'd met with action.

Sam reached beneath his seat and produced the Luger.

The song on the radio changed, and Hayes began to whistle along with a lonesome harmonica. Sam checked the pistol to make sure it was loaded—it was missing two rounds—and rested it alongside his right thigh. Sam watched the red pickup for a few minutes and found he couldn't keep silent. "I keep thinking about those dogs," he said, "what you told me."

"The war dogs?"

"That's right."

"It's a bad thing to kill a dog. Something about it... I never got used to doing that. They wait for you in your dreams."

Sam said, "How many dogs you think it takes to add up to one man?"

"What are you saying?"

"How many dogs do you have to kill for all their lives to equal one man?"

Hayes caressed the shotgun, inhaled deeply before answering. "You know, I think it's one-to-one, Sam. You kill a dog and it's just like killing a man. Life is life, and it's hard to make a case for one over the other. Maybe that's the reason for the dreams."

I guess that fits, Sam thought, *because some men are dogs.*

»»»»»

Sam's dream—the one he had again and again—was a tall tale. It began with bits of truth, but as each dream moment unraveled, it skewed further and further from reality.

The bits of truth: his father, and a black heart in the man's hands as he marched toward the hottest of suns. And then the dream dovetailed into fantasy. A gun in Sam's hands. An assault rifle. The tight fit of combat boots around his feet. The dead weight of body armor and rations, ammunition dangling from his shoulders like prison chains. And Sam moved through a tight desert alley, a long open tunnel between two rows of bleached homes. He led four men—Hayes, Ryder, Sam's adult son and his own father. The men lurked behind him, moved like shadows in their combat gear. Every so often—as the group moved in formation through the alley—Sam heard whispers, muted accusations. "He doesn't know," came one. "What's he doing?" came another. "Let's shoot his ass." That was Ryder. But Sam kept moving, placed one boot in front of the other, came out into a small clearing with a water basin—as big around as a kiddie pool—and two mangy dogs licking from the black, putrid water. He saw two children, a boy and a girl, playing in the dirt beside the basin. The children were naked, and Sam saw dark splotches rubbed into their skin. With his men behind him, Sam scanned the clearing, caught a pair of eyes in one window—he discharged his weapon. The gunfire erupted for a brief moment, echoed. It was not a strange sound here. The rounds plunged into cinder block, left holes the size of tiny fists. More whispers from his men, accusations he didn't understand. And Sam heard snarling, insane and jagged snarling. He turned to see the two dogs—*no*, he thought, *mangy coyotes*—running hard at him. Both animals were jacked with rage. Their muscles bulged through matted fur. Their eyes shone with hatred. Sam swung his gun on them, opened up... The rounds plunged through fur, through skin, through hard lithe muscle—two simultaneous shrieks racked his ears. Both coyotes fell in gray lumps at Sam's feet. And as he stared down at them, his assault rifle giving off small funnels of heat, Sam felt the presence of four men alongside him. He looked left and right, counted four pairs of beige, dirt-crusted combat boots.

It was then, always and forever then, that Sam awoke from his dream and saw the light he knew so well.

21

At first, Jazz headed west on the highway. It looked like he planned to make house calls. It was winter break for the local high school, and he knew, or Sam figured he knew, that he'd find a few boys at home with their parents. Sam knew from all those times out drinking with the man: Jazz always met in person if he could—it put him as a face in the parents' minds. Harder to discount someone if you knew them on a personal level.

Before he reached the main drag in town, Jazz slowed the truck, drifted into the center lane, and whipped the steering wheel to his left. He veered onto the soft, sandy shoulder, but gave it enough gas to shoot forward onto the highway. As Hayes tried to slow the Dodge, Sam watched the red truck blur past them, bleached desert sprawled as a backdrop. "You better flip us around."

"No shit." Hayes hit the brakes, caught the wheel with one hand, and pulled a tight U-turn on the highway. When the Dodge came around, he slapped his own chest twice—quick, rapid like gunfire—and floored the throttle. His cheek muscles churned beneath his skin. "What's he doing?"

"I don't know. How could I know?" Sam stared after the red Chevy. The Dodge kept pace, though Hayes kept them a hundred yards or so to the rear. Traffic was light on the four-lane road, most of it headed the opposite direction, pickups and dusty sedans with cracked windshields on their way back into town. "I guess he knows we're following him—that's for damn sure."

"Well, now that he knows, we might as well keep going."

"How much gas do you have?"

"Full tank, or so the gauge promises. If he stops, we stop."

"He'll stop."

"I don't know," Hayes said, and dropped one hand into his

lap. The other he kept latched to the steering wheel. "What's he doing?"

They ran across a flat expanse where the road gave way to white sands spread blanket-like until reaching the fat, low-slung bellies of distant hills—a bowl-like dry lake bed. The Chevy and the Dodge kept heading east along the highway and, through the windshield, Sam traced the orange sun as it rose—burning ceaseless, yet void of heat—toward and through bulbous, textured clouds. They reached another town, and Sam caught the dull makings of a lonesome gas station. A sheriff's patrol car sat at one pump. He turned to watch, but the patrol car didn't merge onto the highway. They passed a ramshackle assortment of faded pastel buildings. A salon, a small library, three or four cafés and greasy-spoon restaurants. The desert unraveled again, and the two vehicles kept their distance from each other. Another half hour, and the red Chevy spun onward into the folds of undulating cacti and misshapen boulders.

Sam looked to Hayes, but his friend's eyes were squinted, and Sam imagined he was deep in thought. What were they doing? Following Jazz, for whatever purpose, felt stupid now that they were doing it—Sam did not understand how it was he found himself here, in the passenger seat with a pistol wedged between his legs. *You understood before*, he reminded himself. *It was something about what Ryder did to you, and what Jazz did to Hayes. It was all about manhood. Wasn't it? Forget it, Sam... Life is about letting go of everything and embracing the nothing.*

Right. The nothing.

The road grew pockmarked and water wrecked. Through the floorboards, dull throbs touched Sam's feet and left him craving a solid surface on which to place his feet. To the southwest, he saw thin clouds forming over round-topped foothills. When the highway rotated northward, Sam pivoted his gaze, and sunlight penetrated the distant clouds. He saw straight lines of mist punching down through the atmosphere—sheets of rain.

Ahead, the red Chevy kept on toward the highway's tapered

endpoint, an endpoint that Sam knew would keep unraveling like a ball of black, insensitive yarn. The desert brush changed, grew more sparse. He counted chollas for a long while and, when he grew bored, switched to following—with one eye closed—the thin barbed wire along the road's edge. He wondered about the fencing. Why barbed wire here, this far into the desert? Maybe animals—there were deer, he knew, and coyotes and bobcats and bighorn sheep. The road twisted back south, and Sam closed his eyes for a few minutes. He waited until he heard Hayes sigh before saying, "How long are we going to follow him?"

"I want to know what he's doing."

"I think he's wondering what we're doing."

"I told you what it is."

Yes, it's murder. What did they call it? *Pre-meditated,* Sam recalled. He opened his eyes, watched the truck's bumper bounce with the road, ascend and descend into spacious dips, power through hairpin curves. All the while, Hayes gave chase; his concentration did not waver. The desert screamed by Sam's vision, and he wondered: *How many deaths are there in a simple, small-town life?*

Before Today

In the cinder-block cabin, Ryder crumpled against the thin carpet. A series of surprised gasps flew from his mouth. The rifle dangled from one arm, and his gaze burned into Sam. "I didn't think you'd do it," he said. The words came out half formed, shells of themselves. "I didn't think you could. I thought, the pansy don't have it in him."

Sam stood and walked toward the man. For a moment, he paused, took in the sight of Ryder folded up like a misshapen paper crane. He bent down and yanked the rifle away from him. He tossed it onto the futon and hovered over the man like a storm cloud. A black splotch of blood seeped from Ryder's belly, through his flannel, and ran down into the crotch of his Levi's.

Sam said, "I don't know if you're religious."

Ryder moved his lips, but no sound came.

"I guess that took your breath away, huh?"

Ryder tried again. "I grew up Catholic."

"You know some prayers?"

Ryder didn't answer. His chest moved rapidly in and out. His throat gurgled. He tried to sit up, managed to push himself onto one elbow.

"I'm going to help you stand up, old man," Sam said. "You and me are going outside." *Into the valley of death*, Sam thought. *Where you'll be buried.*

The men left two sets of footprints in the snow, one more distinct than the other. Sam dragged Ryder much of the way. The old man was skinny as a rail, easy to pull along, like dragging a bundle of broken tree branches. They reached the center of Ryder's property. The land had been cleared, and it was surrounded by a rough rectangle of desert brush. Where they stood, it was flat and thick with snow. Sam let Ryder fall to the ground. He said, "Where do you keep your tools, old man? Looks like we're going to need a shovel."

»»»»

When Sam got back, Ryder had dragged himself toward the line of Joshua trees and yucca plants. He'd made it a few feet, but there was still some fifty yards or so before he reached cover. "You're not going to make it, Ryder," Sam said. "I'm sorry about that."

Sam gripped the shovel as tightly as he could. His hand screamed with pain that ached into his wrist and shoulder. He told himself: *You've got to do it, pain be damned. Man up for once in your life, Sam.* He plunged the shovel through snow and deep into the sand. He bent at the knees, scooped, and tossed the sand behind him. His hand throbbed, but he plunged the shovel into the sand again, scooped, tossed. He tightened his grip on the wooden handle.

And he did it again.

And again.

And again.

Ryder scraped at the snow, pulled himself—inch by endless inch—toward the place where his land met desert. Blood poured from his stomach. Behind him, a rouge trail appeared like smoke, but unlike smoke, it didn't fade.

Sam scooped one last mound of dirt, tossed it onto the large pile he'd made. He turned and threw the shovel onto the pile. From the corner of his eye, he caught movement. He turned and squinted. Near the cabin, a lone coyote moved into the clearing. The animal's head was hunched low to the ground and his tail was pointed straight down, as if signaling the direction to hell. There it is, the tail said, right under your feet. Sam watched as the coyote crept forward, studied the scene, and darted back into the desert. He heard coyote calls. A chorus of cackles and half-formed howls—the pack wanted food.

Coyotes, Sam thought, *they're so damn nosy.*

"You-you got a witness now," Ryder said. His voice was weak and scratchy. His chest heaved as he tried to laugh. Blood caked at the corners of his mouth, ran down his chin in spurts. "You watch, that-that coyote... He'll turn you in, boy. I just, I bet. Witness to a crime."

Sam walked toward Ryder and stood over him. The old man's skin was pasty, see-through as parchment. The wrinkles in his face were less pronounced, as if the skin were giving up its hold on the old man's bones. Sam leaned over and grabbed Ryder by his bone-thin ankles. "Come on."

"No, boy. Don't you do it... I need—"

"Shut up, old man." Sam dragged Ryder back along his smeared trail of blood and gave one big heave—the old man tumbled into the hole.

Ryder howled with pain. He tried to get air, gulped with his mouth wide open, and slumped into a ball. His eyes went blank for an instant, but came back to life as the pain subsided. "God Almighty," he said. "Good Lord in hell."

Sam watched without flinching. He touched the scar along his chin. The raised skin was warm, a ribbon of heat through the nerves on his face. Sam took himself back to the moment when he'd awoken in the Dodge after being pistol-whipped by Ryder. He'd seen Hayes there first, a detached look on his face. It was still a boy's face, but who knew what it would be when Hayes got back home, if he ever did make it back home. That was a time before all this, before more than nothing became Sam's life, and before less than more was how he felt. *Memories are phantoms*, he thought, *lost to time*. His memory of Hayes faded, merged with the image of the old man's slumped body in a shallow grave. He said, "If there's anything wrong with your boy when he gets back, it's you that did it. It isn't this world, or the one over there." He lifted a finger and jabbed it at the old man. "It's you that did it." Sam tasted stale breath in his mouth, a stink in his throat. "You're fading smoke."

"You think he'll let you get away with this?" Ryder's eyes closed. He pushed more words from his throat. "You think my boy will let you get away with this? He's a killer now, and a killer don't let vengeance ride. You're a dead man."

Sam looked toward the horizon and swiveled his gaze across the desert. There were high clouds above them now and the sun was hidden. The snow wouldn't melt before nightfall. *Hell, it might even snow again tonight*, he thought. He hoped so. That'd make things easier to arrange here at the cabin. He needed to move the old man's stuff out, get rid of it. *I'll make it seem like he ran off, headed to wherever the hell a no-good old man heads to. Far off, that's where. And the International pickup? I'll burn the fucker.* He looked back to the old man. "Well then," he said. "Time to get this show on the road. I need to be home for dinner." Sam lifted the shovel, grimaced as fiery pain coursed through his hand and arm. He scooped some dirt and tossed it onto Ryder's face.

The old man didn't flinch.

»»»»»

As he rode along in the roaring Dodge Dart, Sam felt the pulse of the Luger in his palm, how it had spat at Ryder. He saw again the surprised look on the man's face, how he'd fallen downward like a sheet from a clothesline—blood seeping from his chest, dark and splotchy. And the war dogs—Sam thought about how many Hayes had killed, whether they added up to one man's father or whether they were forgotten, forgivable, forgettable. He pulled himself upward in his seat, squinted into the flat sky where it was growing bruised with ominous cloud cover. "I think we'll hit rain. Looks like a downpour, too."

"If we hit it, he hits it. He's got to stop at some point."

The vehicles swung onward across the black tarmac. Hayes hummed a tune to himself. Sam watched as Hayes tapped out a beat on the steering wheel, tilted his knee up and down with the soft, vinyl-toned thump.

They hit the rain faster than Sam expected. Arrow-shaped raindrops pelted the windshield, smacked the thin sheen of water on the road. Hayes gripped the wheel with both hands, clenched his jaw so the muscles in his cheeks flexed, fleshy as prunes. The truck seemed hidden behind a veil. Sam leaned forward and squinted, tried to follow the blinking taillights as Jazz braked for bends and flooded portions of the highway. "Not so fast," he said.

Hayes nodded and sighed. "I got it. Don't worry."

Sam clutched the pistol tighter, rubbed his chapped lips together. The rain came harder, and Sam sensed Hayes tapping the brakes as they hydroplaned once or twice across patchy sections of the road. They had seen few cars coming from the opposite direction. If they crashed here, Sam knew there was little chance someone would see them—this meant bad news if they were injured. For the first time since that morning, with a tinge of shame, Sam thought of Reagan and Erin waiting for him back home. He hadn't called Erin. Now that morning was stretching into middle day, she had no idea where he was, what he was doing. Was this day to be another of his failures? Like yesterday in the bedroom? His throat closed and his mouth grew dry. "Slow down, will you?"

"I need to keep up with the fucker or he'll lose us at the junction."

Again, Sam clutched the pistol tight—the steel was warm against his hand, and the trigger was slippery with sweat from his fingers. "Fine," Sam said, "go faster. Let's catch him now, while the rain comes. It's coming down now—let's go, faster." He stared hard at the wet road, scratched at the pistol's trigger with one long fingernail. "Faster," he said. "Faster."

22

Ahead, through the rain's gloomy sheets, the truck's taillights flashed red, stuttered, and came on for what seemed a long time. Hayes touched the Dodge's brakes but didn't stop. The highway curled left, split a low-lying wash, and lifted. As they headed toward the wash, the truck's blockish shape raised itself and stopped, jutted from the rain like a ghost. Jazz had gone through the wash, hit the rushing water, and power-slid to a halt on the other side. The driver's side of the truck faced back toward the wash, and inside, Jazz's beady eyes hovered. Hayes mashed the brake pedal with his entire foot and said, "Holy shit, man. Hold on tight."

In the passenger seat, Sam's voice spilled loud and frantic, "Watch out!"

They hit the water and brown mud exploded onto the windows. Hayes let off the brakes—that might help him control the Dodge—and punched the throttle. As they came out of the wash and headed skyward, the Dodge's rear tires skimmed the road, unclenched their hold, and the car rotated to the left, with its nose pointed northward. He mashed the brakes once more and the car scraped to a stop. "That was fun," Hayes said, and looked at Sam.

Sam turned to the window. He hunched forward slightly and tilted his chin upward—his forehead bumped against the glass. "There you are, you rat." He lifted the Luger from his lap, touched its barrel to the window. His heart thumped in his chest.

Sam wondered: *Why in the hell am I so excited?*

The truck's tires spun against wet pavement, and Jazz nosed the truck onto the highway shoulder. His clean-shaven cheeks appeared through the windshield, and below them, the pressed shirt draped across his shoulders.

Hayes spoke. "You got all dressed up for your funeral, didn't you?"

The truck veered west, spit wet sand onto the Dodge's hood, and rejoined the highway.

"Let's go, dammit." Sam lowered the Luger and then, for an instant, lifted it in the general direction of the truck. "Hurry up." He dropped the Luger back into his lap and cleared his throat. "Don't let him lose us."

»»»»»

They came out of the rain about twenty minutes later. Dark clouds parted to the north, exposed a solitary shard of blue, like flesh from a knife wound. The desert looked more green to Sam, as if the shrubbery opened itself and drank from the sky. He watched two solitary birds—black as flies—twist and dive around each other. The highway continued its cruel unraveling—the red Chevy pulled them onward into the desert. He felt as though his fate was lashed to Hayes, and to the Marine driving the red truck. There was a hole in each of them and, through each hole, a cord ran as hard and tight as an electric line from one steel tower to the next. Anger: It burned through him and Hayes like electricity, was zipped from one man to the other, a ceaseless exchange of power, diminished only by their being apart. But now they were together, and Sam felt the anger course through him.

"The junction's coming up—which way you think he'll go?"

Sam said, "He'll head toward Interstate ten, where there's more people."

"We have to stop him before he gets there, take him off the road." Hayes sighed after he spoke. His fingers curled around the steering wheel, thin and white with tension.

Silence hung between them. Sam bit his bottom lip and tried to count the yellow dashes running down the highway's center. How would they stop Jazz? And the biggest question: If they did stop him, would they go through with it—would Hayes kill him?

"If you get closer, I can try to shoot one of his tires."

"Are you any good with a pistol?"

This pressed a smile to Sam's lips, but he pushed it down, hid it. "Probably not that good." He shouldn't be smiling at his own prowess with a pistol—it took nothing to shoot a man at point-blank range. Well, nothing besides the guts. And a cruel, twisted fear. Skill was beside the point, a secondary consideration.

"Thought so."

"So, what?"

"At the junction, when he stops, I'll just pull in front of him. If we get out fast enough, you can pull him out and—"

"Shoot him?"

Hayes shook his head. "I want that part."

"Look at us," Sam said, "regular outlaws."

Hayes didn't reply, and the yellow dashes began running smooth down the highway's center. Its path now wound upward into a brief range of foothills. Sam had taken this road enough— three, four times—to know the junction was just beyond the hills, along with a decrepit gas station and a few sun-bleached homesteads. *That's when,* he thought. *That's when we'll get him. It'll be at the gas station, or just before—I'll have to smack him as hard as I can, put him out cold, or he'll put up a fight.*

»»»»»»

Coming down out of the hills, the red Chevy truck whipping in and out of his sight, Sam's heart thumped a ceaseless rhythm. He lifted his left hand and pressed it to his chest. The hills receded as the Dodge Dart spun toward the desert floor. The road swung in half revolutions, first south and then north, as if they were tying themselves in a knot. Sam's heart pelted his palm. He grunted and lowered his hand, scratched at the worn spot where his left knee poked through his Levi's.

Hayes said, "You okay, buddy?"

"Fine. I just feel like my heart is going to pop."

"Make sure it holds on for a little longer." He glanced at Sam from the corner of one eye.

Sam ignored him, turned his stare to the winding road. It curled through stands of juniper, descended into flighty patches of cholla and creosote—Sam noticed the sands shift from a deep brown to a light beige. "I'll hold on as long as it takes," Sam said. His heart kept pumping, a fist curling and releasing inside his body, a flower blooming and giving up on life. He took a few deep breaths and gripped the Luger.

As the road tilted northward, the truck disappeared from view at the next bend. It was a long sweeping turn, and Hayes cursed behind the wheel. The Dodge's engine roared as he plowed through the bend. The suspension creaked beneath them, and Sam pressed his hand into the seat to keep from losing his balance.

Ahead, the road began to settle back into a straight line, but as they crested a slight rise, Sam and Hayes caught sight of the truck at the same time—it was parked crossways in the highway. Standing in front of the truck, a small black object in his right hand, was Jazz. His beige uniform shirt and crisp slacks rippled in the wind. His mouth was screwed into a comma, and the muscles in his cheeks flexed.

Hayes applied the brakes. His voice was gravel and glass: "This son of a gun sure does have some balls. I didn't expect this, I'll admit it."

As the Dodge slowed, Sam watched Jazz's hand tighten around the black object. It was, Sam could tell, a pistol. The Dodge stopped. It sat on the highway, hunched and lethal looking, pointed at Jazz, with white puffs of loose smoke spitting from its tailpipe. Hayes flipped the ignition and the desert's uncanny silence filled the air.

Hayes and Sam exited the car.

Both men stood in the highway, their hair flapping in the light wind. Sam held the Luger at his side. Hayes, his mouth twisting uncontrollably beneath his angled nose, carried the pump-action

Remington. The air was wet from the rain, and Sam licked at it from the corner of his mouth. He tried to focus on anything but the rogue piston-fire of his heart. *I need to slow myself,* he thought, *or my heart will beat me to death.*

Jazz cleared his throat and said, "I just want to get it over with."

"Better to face the music, as they say."

Sam heard Hayes speak, though his voice sounded distant and hollow.

Jazz looked down at the pistol in his hand. He shrugged. "I use this for target practice, and that's all it was ever for."

Sam felt along the Luger's trigger guard. He traced the sensual curve of the trigger with a thin finger, tilted the pistol upward and, as if it were a half-filled shadow from a dream, saw his gnarled right hand hover into view. He said, "I did it once before, and now I have to do it again." For a moment, his hand panned downward, wavered in its certainty, but he steadied himself and centered the pistol on Jazz's head.

Hayes pumped the shotgun, lifted it to his right shoulder. "It's not you who gets to do it, Sam. I'm the one, I'm the one who has to do it."

Jazz did not lift the pistol. He appeared stunned and, Sam thought, resigned to his own destiny. Sam closed one eye, glared through the Luger's sights. He could see Jazz's head there, pin shaped and miniature, but Sam's eye closed on itself, went black against the stale blue sky and sunlight.

Hayes said, "Sam? Sam?"

Sam came back, pulled himself from the black hole, pressed the darkness to the edges of his vision. *What is this? What's happening to me?* The piston fired in his chest and a flame-like sensation spread from his heart to his shoulder, seeped into the bottom of his throat. Sam's arm panned downward again. He squinted and aimed at Jazz's shiny black boots. *I'll get his feet, knock the son of a gun onto his ass. That's what I'll do.* "I'm going to kill you," he said, but did not comprehend that it was a whisper over his lips. "I'm going to knock you on your ass, you son of a gun."

"Sam? What the hell is wrong with you?"

Jazz said, "It's happening to him again."

Hayes stepped toward Jazz and said, "You stay right there." Turning to Sam, Hayes lifted his chin and squinted. "Come on back, buddy. I'm right here with you. Come on back now."

Sam's vision cleared and he pinned his eyes to Hayes. *You're a war hero*, he thought. *A little punk who grew up to be a war hero—who in the hell would have thought that? Why not me? If it was you, why not me?* He studied, again, the blue-black bruise on one side of Hayes's face. "You did this to me," Sam said. "It was you."

Hayes lowered the Remington, his face crushed into a perplexed expression. Beneath his coat, his shoulders broadened. "What in the hell are you talking about, Sam? Is this more of your flower talk?"

The last phrase perked Sam's senses. Three times now he'd heard that. He was still conscious of the Luger in his hand, though it had fallen to aim at the pavement. "It was you who stopped him." He motioned to Jazz. "You told him not to take me, you said so yesterday—said you offered yourself instead of me."

Jazz said, "That's true. He did."

"Shut up, Jazz." Sam waved the Luger at him—dismissive—and swung it to Hayes. Blue sky wavered above him. He narrowed his eyes and focused on the hawk-like nose and shotgun eye sockets. He thought: *An engine's got no say when it goes—they say life is a gift, and it is.* "You remember we stole that truck, Hayes? The Ford? You remember that?"

"I remember, buddy. You were afraid—"

"I wasn't afraid of anything!" Sam licked his lips. "I wasn't afraid. Don't you say that. You ran that truck into the ground. Kept on the thing until it gave up. A good truck and you just, what? You destroy it for no good reason?"

"We were just kids. We were having fun."

"You call that fun—destruction?"

"That's what kids do, Sam. It's natural—hell, it's expected."

"What's *expected*. That's an interesting subject." Sam laughed and he heard in himself a deep madness, a thing upended somewhere out of reach. "You're right. For men, it's destruction that's expected." Sam nodded and shuffled toward Hayes. He felt the Dodge's hot grill at his hip. "You go around and destroy whatever you can get your hands on. That's exactly what's expected."

"You're coming at me with a pistol," Hayes said. He lifted the Remington slightly, as if poking it into a snake's den. "Stop waving that thing at me, Sam."

Everything is wrong with me, Sam thought. *Everything is all twisted up and used again and again.* He tried with all his strength to lower the pistol, but it kept coming up, raising itself. His squinting eye traced flapping denim Levi's, a slim torso covered by a military-green coat, stopped on the hawk-like nose, where it was rigid against smooth white skin. *In the chest, I'll get him in the chest.* A will to fire the pistol ached within him, and Sam pushed this ache from the depths of his mind, down through his arm, and into the gnarled nerves of his misshapen right hand. Along his chin, the thin purple scar throbbed.

Sam fired the Luger.

His muscles slackened. A flame seared in his chest, gripped the upper reaches of his throat, spread downward into his left elbow, the place where his ribs met flabby belly. *A flower inside me*, Sam thought. *All these things will bloom*, he thought. *Will the world shrink around me? Will the stars surge against my face, my head, my skin?*

In that moment, while a harsh burn seared through his body, while his best friend was crumpled on the black pavement, Sam thought of his son: He saw a little boy's vague blue eyes stretch into the years, reflect against desert landscapes unfolding as if pastel images tossed against wind. *How will you live without me? How will you eat and breathe and drink?*

From the fountain, Sam thought. *All the fountains in the world are for my son to drink from.*

He did not understand his thoughts, or the blind obedience of his finger—*that tiny, thin finger should not have obeyed me,* he thought. His vision cleared for a brief instant. He saw Hayes's face centered in the gunsights. His mouth worked upward against his nose. Those shotgun eyes pointed at Sam and—after how long Sam couldn't tell—closed on themselves. *There,* Sam thought. *There he was before me, and all I could do was fire the pistol. It's him,* Sam told himself. *It's him. It's him. It's me. It's only ever me.*

And Hayes's face darkened, dimmed, vanished.

Reagan's face came into Sam's head again. A smooth, fleshy face with those blue eyes and a mouth open in hunger. Or thirst. *My son,* Sam thought, *will drink from this world.*

And the burn exploded in his chest. Sam opened his mouth, heard a loose grunt rattle from his throat, and clenched his eyes as the burn warped the inside of his head. *I'm me,* he thought. *It's me.* The last thing he saw before collapsing beside Hayes— wide and open and wonderful—was the gaping mouth of blue sky above him. From one corner, a hint of cloud cover moved like saliva. It was a pure sight, innocent and vibrant and awash in soft hues.

I'm me, he thought. *It's me.*

And Sam lost consciousness.

23

Sam tied his grease-stained apron behind his back. He tapped a steel spatula against the flat-top grill and waited for Nelson to unlock the diner's door. On the grill, rows of fat-laced bacon sizzled. "How was business on my days off, Nelson? You keep up with the orders? Or did you miss me?"

Nelson ambled toward the glass front door and, to unlock it, inserted a brass key. He shrugged, and a series of short coughs boomed from his throat. He slid the key back into his pocket and sat at the diner counter. "Sunday I got behind on omelets. Those damn holy rollers rushed us, and we couldn't do nothing about it. I was thinking I can't make those to order on Sundays, should probably have the eggs cracked and ready. What do you think?"

Sam slid the spatula beneath a row of bacon, flipped the pieces with precise violence. He'd done this so many times over the years. "I think that'll make it easier. What you might do is run a Sunday special. A sandwich, something you can put together real fast. That's the way to go."

"It'll have to be cheap if we want the old folks to bite."

"Misers, aren't they? Think they own the world, too."

"Yeah, well—we need them to keep this place going."

Sam said, "I'm not complaining." He flipped another row of bacon, set the spatula down, and turned his hand upward, studied the lines on his mangled palm. *Like my heart,* he thought. *And maybe my mind.* "Just saying, that's all."

"Say," Nelson said, "you run up to see your buddy?"

Sam nodded. He turned to Nelson and placed his palms on the counter, leaned forward as if to tell a secret. "I did, yeah. I have to say, I mean, I shouldn't say this—he's kind of, you know..."

"Shit, what is it?"

"He's got the head thing, the shakes or whatever."

Nelson shook his head. "You saying Hayes is messed up in the head, Sam?" He squinted, his fat cheeks pushing into his eye sockets. "Like what they say in the news and all?"

"I'm saying, things aren't normal up there." Sam tapped his head with a finger. "That's all. I got nothing more than that." He went back to the grill and slid the spatula beneath the bacon. He set the pieces off to the side and pressed another sheet to the grill. Fat and grease sizzled.

"What's Hayes going to do?"

"What do you mean?"

"For work?"

Sam paused and looked back at Nelson. "Oh, he's not looking for work right now. Probably won't be for a long while."

"You tell him he's got a job here if he wants it. I don't care if he shakes himself to hell and back. He's got a job here after what he did."

"I'll tell him," Sam said. "Next time I see him."

Nelson stood, surveyed the empty diner and walked toward his office. "The girl called and said she'd be a little late."

"I'll take care of the place until she gets here. No worries."

"Alright then," Nelson said.

He shut the door behind him and left Sam alone to his own work and thoughts. *No*, Sam thought, *Hayes won't be looking for work any time soon, or ever. Hayes won't be looking for anything ever again.* As he watched bacon sizzle on the grill, Sam thought of Hayes, but in his mind he did not see a man. He saw a smiling kid with a round face, a kid who had scratched a near-curse word into a desk. He saw the teenager who helped him dig holes for two dead dogs, the not-quite-man who piled soft dirt onto the rotten, forgotten carcasses. He saw a boy becoming a man, but not the man himself. And that was, he thought, the way it should be—*we are always, in death, the promise of what we could have been.*

First lies the father, Sam thought, *and second lies the son.*

Sam lifted a piece of hot bacon from the grill, bit into it like a hungry dog. Bacon grease scorched his tongue, but he chewed and chewed and chewed, forced the meat down his throat. *So damn good,* he thought. And that was the extent of his thinking: vague, flitting assertions about bacon and over-easy eggs, and the ceaseless churning of ten thousand days and nights.

A few minutes later, when Jazz came in for his breakfast, he didn't look shocked or grieved or at all different. There was a dead look in his eyes—a look that said nothing. Sam nodded at him, reached across the counter and shook hands with the man.

Jazz settled himself at the counter, smoothed down the collar of his clean-pressed shirt, and eyeballed the bacon. "You mind giving me a piece of that?"

Sam slid a few pieces onto a white plate, set it on the counter. "We'll get you some coffee, too."

"I could use some cream and sugar."

"Cream and sugar," Sam said. "God knows, we couldn't live without it."

»»»»»

Desert weeds pierced the soil in places, but he made out the circular section where he'd filled Ryder's grave.

Sam lifted the shovel and plunged it into the dirt.

I am going to dig you up, you son of a gun.

He threw the dirt behind him, plunged the shovel deeper into the earth.

I am going to find every last bone.

Again, Sam tossed the dirt and jammed the shovel back into the grave.

And I am going to bury your son beside you.

Toss. Plunge.

Soldiers of the heartland, buried together like brothers.

Toss. Plunge.

I am going to give you your son's bones, old man.

Toss. Plunge.

And I will forget about you both forever.

Toss. Plunge.

You see, I have a boy to raise, a man to build.

Toss. Plunge.

I have a world in this dust, and I have a boy who needs me to show him what it means to live.

Beneath the metallic bite of his shovel, the hole deepened.

Acknowledgements

I first want to thank my wife, Lesley, and my son, Charlie, for the constant fun and inspiration. And especially for those times when you make space for me to write. It's slow going sometimes, but it happens...A special thanks to Jeff Sirkin, Tim Z. Hernandez, and Marion Rohrleitner—professors and writers at the University of Texas at El Paso who read the earliest versions of this book and provided invaluable feedback. A second massive thank you to Jeff Sirkin for pushing me beyond my own barriers as a writer. I want to thank Krysta Winsheimer for the incredible editorial perspective and expertise. This book benefits deeply from Krysta's developmental and narrative expertise—I couldn't finish the book without her dedication. I want to thank writer-editor Vern Smith at Run Amok Books for the support and humor and belief in my work. Thank you, man...Thanks also to Gary Anderson at Run Amok Books for the production support and making it all happen. I need to thank the writers JD Clapp, Joel Nedecky, Jo Perry, Thomas Trang, Alec Cizak, AB Patterson, and Vern Smith... You all keep me going in the face of massive obstacles to the independent artist. Please, keep doing your work...And I'll keep doing mine—I promise. And to the reader, wherever you are. Thank you for caring about the great power of novels, and for spending time with my unique, authentic words and thoughts.

About the Author

Matt Phillips lives in San Diego. His novels include the Thriller Award Finalist *A Good Rush of Blood*, as well as *Countdown, Know Me From Smoke, To Bring My Shadow, You Must Have A Death Wish, Three Kinds of Fool*, and the short story collection *Quiet and the Darkness*.